N

THE
WOODLAND
REALM

☆ARAVIO

E MINES

☆CRAEWICK

THE STONE REALM

SEA

PRAISE FOR LAUREN MANSY

AND *THE MEMORY THIEF*

"*The Memory Thief* is a thought-provoking debut full of unique magic and complex characters. Lauren Mansy is definitely an author to watch!"

—EVELYN SKYE, *New York Times* Bestselling author of
The Crown's Game series and *Circle of Shadow*

"*The Memory Thief* is a vivid story full of surprising twists and turns. An exciting, riveting debut!"

—REBECCA ROSS, author of *The Queen's
Rising* and *The Queen's Resistance*

"An entrancing story-world of memory heists, hidden maze-prisons, and unexplored magic. *The Memory Thief* kept me second-guessing with every shocking revelation and daring to believe that the journey to healing is worth the trials of heartache to get there."

—NADINE BRANDES, author of *Romanov*

THE
MEMORY
THIEF

THE
MEMORY
THIEF

LAUREN MANSY

BLINK®

BLINK

The Memory Thief
Copyright © 2019 by Lauren Mansy

Requests for information should be addressed to:
Blink, *3900 Sparks Dr. SE, Grand Rapids, Michigan 49546*

Hardcover ISBN 978–0–310–76765–7

ITPE ISBN 978-0-310-76979-8

Audio ISBN 978-0-310-76856-2

Ebook ISBN 978-0-310-76757-2

Interior design: Denise Froehlich

Printed in the United States of America

---

19 20 21 22 23   LSC   10 9 8 7 6 5 4 3 2 1

A12007 371647

For my family.

GLOSSARY OF TERMS

Gifted are those with the ability to transfer memory from one mind to another through touch. They can detect another Gifted by the energy which radiates from a Gifted's skin, the source which makes the transfer of memory possible.

Ungifted can receive foreign memories but cannot transfer memories themselves. They're often the victims of memory theft and wear many layers of clothing to protect their skin. Most of the Ungifted work in the city of Craewick as farmers, blacksmiths, masons, tailors, and carpenters.

Sifters are the most powerful of the Gifted, having the ability to transfer memories through sight. Sifters rule each of the Four Realms, and the rarity of their Gift makes them the most respected and feared of the Gifted. A Sifter can implant memories quickly enough to change one's thoughts in an instant and steal enough memories to kill with a single glance. The large amount of energy in their skin creates a barrier around their minds which protects their memories from being stolen by another Sifter. One trait all Sifters share is the gold flecks in their eyes, a sign of the extra energy of their Gift.

The **Minders** are the Four Realms' army, a large battalion of Gifted soldiers. Most of the Gifted are conscripted into the Minders, unless they come from wealthy families who can pay to opt out of service.

Collectors are the Gifted who work for the Craewick Treasury. They spend years mastering talents throughout the Four Realms and sell them at the Memory Auction or at the treasury.

Hollows are the wealthiest of the Gifted. Because taking on too many foreign memories can muddle the mind, Hollows are known by their graying eyes and dazed looks. They often dress with every inch of skin covered to protect their minds from memory theft.

Shadows are the best thieves in the Four Realms. They run the black market of memories in the Mines, a hidden underground city. The Shadows are a safe haven for orphans and anyone looking to avoid their Minder conscription. Their motto is "to help those who can't help themselves," and they protect the Ungifted, often hunting down Minders who steal from the Ungifted and returning the memories to their rightful owners. They also protect the Ungifted from the Ghosts when the Minders fail to do so.

Ghosts are those who create and implant violent, painful memories. They're usually hired by the Hollows to make an enemy suffer and often attack and steal memories from the Ungifted. Though the Minders consider both groups to be thieves and traitors, the Ghosts and the Shadows are adversaries.

Hunters are those who chose to read and take on memories from the minds of animals. A combination of animal instincts and human nature, they're skilled trackers and often travel in packs.

Ungifted Tribes are large groups of nomadic, Ungifted people who've chosen to live fully apart from the Gifts.

THE FOUR REALMS

The Stone Realm is ruled by Madame in the capital city of Craewick. The largest of the four allied Realms, it is a trading post which supplies the other Realms with tangible goods crafted by the large population of Ungifted workers who live in Craewick.

The Desert Realm is ruled by Declan in the capital city of Kripen. It is the military base for the Minders, known for its many taverns, rowdy citizens, and brutal training methods.

The Coastal Realm is ruled by Sorien in the capital city of Blare. It is where all the arts, from painting to singing to dancing, are taught.

The Woodland Realm is ruled by Porter in the capital city of Aravid. It is where the sciences, mathematics, and histories are taught.

CHAPTER 1

When I see the letter nailed to my door, I know something is terribly wrong.

The envelope is covered in fancy handwriting and sealed with a wax stamp the color of dried blood. I don't wonder who it's from because only the Minders use red ink—and they never send good news.

I shove the letter under my cloak, hoping no one on the crowded streets has seen what the peacekeepers have sent me. My hands tremble so badly that it takes a few tries to fit my key in the lock. As a chill works its way through my bones, I twist the iron handle, walk in, and shut the door to my cottage. I sit before my legs give out, pulling my cloak around me.

My throat tightens at the warm scents of honey and

violets buried in the wool. The last time my mother wore this was the day before she entered the asylum, almost four years ago. Somehow, it still smells like her.

A knock on the door jolts me.

"Etta?"

The door opens slightly as Ryder slips inside. Even in the dim light, the bruise blooming near her left eye is hard to miss, and her lip is cracked and bloody. But I'm not surprised. She's spent the last few hours on the street corners, where the crowds are as restless as the prisoners up for bid tonight.

After all, it's Auction Day.

She slides down beside me, close enough that our shoulders meet. The gold buttons on her tattered jacket catch the last rays of sunlight sneaking in through the grimy window above my copper sink.

Pushing myself to my feet, I resist the urge to tell Ry to be more careful on days like today, reminding myself she isn't a child anymore. I set the envelope down on the floor beside her, walk to the water basin at the edge of the table, and dip a rag into the cool water.

"Is that letter from the Minders?" she asks.

I nod, offering the dripping cloth to her, but she doesn't take it. "Your lip is bleeding, Ry. The cold will help."

"I don't care about my lip." Her eyes are on the envelope. "You didn't open it."

"Because I already know what it is," I say, taking in a deep breath. "It's the lottery ticket for my mother's bed."

Her eyes widen. "The asylum filled up again?"

"I can't believe it either," I whisper.

I knew the rules when I admitted my mother. Each patient is assigned a number, and when the asylum gets overcrowded, the Minders draw slips of paper to choose a patient to kick out. But I never expected it would be my mother. Not after the price I paid to get her in.

Now the Minders will mark an *x* on the end of her bed and transfer any of my mother's memories that I want to keep into me. But because she's so weak, the energy of having her mind read will kill her.

My eyes feel gritty and dry as I stare around the tiny room I rent from the Minders. On the wall across from me, I hung the portraits I sketched of my mother. There are dozens of pictures, all drawn on bits of paper I scrounged up over the years. Next to those are the dresses I sewed for my mother on a few hooks I nailed to the wall. But if the Minders have anything to say about it, she won't need them anymore.

"They can't kick her out," says Ryder. "Did you tell the nurses she moved her fingers? She's waking up."

"It's out of their control, Ry. The lottery is Minder business." I clench my hands into fists, a rush of heat crawling up my neck at the thought of drawing numbers to determine who lives and who doesn't. The Minders claim my mother's death will be painless and peaceful, but who are they to decide when she takes her last breath? I angle toward Ryder. "Do they expect me to sit back and watch her die?"

"The Etta I know wouldn't do that," Ryder says, a glint in her dark eyes.

"The least I can do is battle the Minders until she wakes up," I say.

"And you won't have to fight them alone."

My anger dissolves into fear as I imagine her challenging the Minders' orders—spitting out words she's bitten back for years. The last thing I need is for the Minders to label Ryder a deviant too. Especially on Auction Day, the very example of how they treat the so-called lawless.

Ry clicks her pocket watch open, one stamped with the seal of Craewick that she swindled off a Minder years ago. "We're going to be late."

"I'm not going to the auction, Ry."

"Why not? Being alone won't help anything." She nudges my arm. "Maybe we can pick up something to bribe the Minders to keep your mother in the asylum. Tons of people will be looking to trade tonight, especially after a few pints of Auction Ale."

It's a clever move on Ryder's end, I'll give her that. But if Minders could be bribed, I would've worked that angle years ago. It's true the ale makes bartering a little smoother, but it also makes the auction crowd rash and jumpy, two things Ry shouldn't have to deal with alone.

I'm trembling as I drag myself over to the sink.

Splashing water on my warm cheeks, I sense Ryder waiting for me to break down, but I won't. Not until I get through the next few hours without flinging myself on the auction block and wringing Madame's neck. Or trying to, anyway. Imagining our ruler, the very person who started the lottery, squirming gives only a moment of satisfaction before reality sets back in.

Ryder opens the door when it's time to go. The auction waits for no one.

Tucking the lottery ticket into my pocket, I follow her onto the moonlit streets, already packed with my neighbors pushing their way to the heart of Craewick. But it's clear from their grim faces they don't attend auctions to make purchases. They go to wish loved ones goodbye. To beg the Minders to let their children or their parents come home.

We take all our shortcuts, dodging between unending rows of rotting wooden homes and crumbling brick cottages. The air smells of burning leaves, and I try to remember the last bonfire I attended. Most living on the fray of Craewick spend their evenings sharing two things: flasks of cider and gossip. I'm usually visiting my mother at the asylum, and by the time I get home, everyone's long gone to bed.

Once the buildings change from whitewashed wood to thick stone, we've reached the center of Craewick. The auction is already swarming with people. The stage, the centerpiece of the square, stands out among Craewick's bland storefronts. It's gray, gray, and more gray everywhere. But most who live here don't even notice. Their memories keep them in whichever place in the past they wish to dwell.

The auction block is a perfect circle. As they say, easy viewing makes for easy bidding. It's probably the prettiest part of Craewick, with how the polished wood shines in the firelight from the lanterns strung around it.

The raised platform is also riddled with intricate carvings. There are four panels, each representing the allied Realms. Surrounded by jagged cliffs and cavernous mountains, Craewick is the capital city of the Stone Realm. Most of the Ungifted live here, making us a trading post of goods with all the seamstresses, carpenters, blacksmiths, and farmers who work for Madame. The Desert Realm, the training base for all the Minders, is represented by dueling swords and steel-tipped arrows. The paintbrushes, music notes, and twirling couples are for the Coastal Realm of the arts. And finally, there's the Woodland Realm, where the sciences, mathematics, and histories are taught deep in the forest region. The carvings are so lifelike, the pages of the books looking as if they're fluttering in the wind.

Whoever designed the stage was a true artist, but once you know what happens up there, the beauty is significantly dulled.

As we pass a Minder checking for citizenship around the perimeter of the square, I hold out my wrist to show my tattoos. The first is the crest of the Stone Realm to signify Madame is the ruler I've pledged to serve. The second is far more important, a marking which distinguishes the Gifted from the Ungifted. My tattoo is a hollow circle to indicate I don't have a Gift.

It's also a lie.

The Minder's stare lingers on me, long enough that Ryder takes one look up at him and smirks.

"This guy bothering you, Etta?"

I smile a little. At twelve-years-old, Ryder's voice is too high, her stature too short to convince anyone I'm the one in need of protection. All that matters is that Ry believes she's ten feet tall, and why squash a courageous spirit before it's grown sturdy roots?

The Minder laughs without a hint of humor. "Hilarious, kid."

Ry winks at me.

I follow her along the edge of the audience, finding a spot near a beggar on the street corner. A group pushes past as we stop, unapologetically elbowing their way toward the stage. You can't bid on one of the auctioned if Madame can't see you.

A man in a long-sleeved, high-necked jacket brushes past the beggar beside us, pausing briefly enough where the untrained eye wouldn't notice the way his fingers

linger on the rough patch of skin on her elbow. He's what
we call a Gifted, having the ability to read another's mind
simply by touching them.

The beggar doesn't flinch, clearly doesn't detect the
energy pulsing through her body like another Gifted
would.

His face lights up, his touch siphoning thoughts from
her head until I let out a sharp whistle, loud enough to jolt
the Ungifted beggar.

As she rushes off, the man turns his beady eyes into
the crowd, and I wait until he catches my gaze to smile.
He clenches his jaw, but this thief would have to be an
idiot to start a fight among so many Minders. He scur-
ries off after giving me a dirty look, and I glance up as a
Minder drags a high-backed metal chair to the center of
the stage.

Behind it stands a row of iron-shackled prisoners.
Immediately, I'm searching for any rebels with whom I
might've done business. It's hard to tell since they're all
dressed in ragged prison garb, and most have their heads
down. All but one—a hard-faced boy whose ribs poke
out under his thin shirt.

I grit my teeth at how pitiful he looks.

It's impossible to see his tattoos from back here, but
I'd bet my right eye it's shaped like a sunburst, indicating
the energy in his skin which makes him Gifted. Unlike
the rest of the prisoners, who tuck their arms into their

thin shifts to cover every inch of bare skin, he stands tall and proud.

It's unusual to see a Gifted on auction, though I'm not sure there's much difference between the number of Ungifted and Gifted lawbreakers. It's just the latter usually gets away with it.

The crowd hushes.

One second Madame isn't anywhere in sight, the next she's standing dead center on the stage. Even the wind quiets down as if it wouldn't dare to intrude upon her entrance.

As head of the Minders of the Stone Realm, Madame spends most of her time training her soldiers, so the only time we really see her is on Auction Day. Her hair is the color of the darkest raven against the gray of her military uniform as she surveys the crowd without a hint of a smile on her pale lips. Madame is striking. Not pretty by any means, but I can't look away, my eyes caught on all her pointy features.

She slowly walks down the row of prisoners, studying each one like an insect caught in her web. I can feel the prisoners' fear even from here. It's in the way the chains rattle on their wrists, how they can't meet her eyes. They all know her face is the last thing they'll see before they die.

Madame angles toward the crowd. "A society is only as strong as the morality of its citizens, and we must protect the wisdom of our past to ensure a prosperous future," she says before facing the prisoners. "You have been given a trial and declared guilty."

I almost laugh. Trial? What a joke. What she really means is a few Minders held these prisoners down while she sifted through their minds.

We're never privy to the details, so who knows what these prisoners actually did before being accused of treason. Perhaps one snatched a loaf of bread to feed her starving children, or another can't pay back his debts to the Minders. A lot of Ungifted use desirable memories to pay for rent on those tiny shacks the Minders have the nerve to call cottages. When there's barely enough food to go around and icy wind seeps through every rotting floorboard, you run out of happy memories pretty quickly. Still, the Minders never forget to come collecting.

"The punishment for these crimes is death," Madame says, angling toward the audience. And just for the tiniest moment, she meets my eyes.

My breath hitches in my throat. I tell myself Madame can't possibly see us back here, but fear slices through me when she narrows her sights on Ryder. I take a step in front of Ry, gently nudging her behind me. When the corners of Madame's lips pull up, in a flicker of a mocking smile, I'm certain she's watching me as closely as I'm watching her.

The lottery ticket burns like fire against my skin. *We made a deal,* I want to scream at her. *You promised my mother wouldn't be harmed. You swore she'd have a place at the asylum until she woke. I gave up everything because I believed you!*

I can almost hear her reply.

What a fool you were to believe me.

Madame blinks twice, her gaze darting away. "Bring forth Kellen Marks."

Ryder ducks around me and asks if I'm okay.

I nod but keep my hand on her shoulder.

The Minders usually have to drag unwilling victims forward, but not Kellen Marks, the boy I noticed earlier. He steps out from the line of prisoners without a moment's hesitation. Two Minders secure his arms to the chair, the sharp rattling of the chains cutting through the stagnant air. Most of the auctioned lack the strength to keep their heads up, but Kellen lifts his chin and stares straight into the audience.

I bite my tongue, wishing I could tell him he is not Craewick's true enemy.

It's Madame who will strip him of his most treasured possessions for breaking her Craewick law. Then this mob will stuff themselves full, buying items that'll be enjoyed for a while then discarded like trash. No, Madame is the real criminal here, not Kellen Marks—she's using her *Gift* to steal his life.

Once he's been secured, she takes her place beside him, her bony hand trailing along his shoulders. "Do you have any last words, Kellen Marks?"

He tips his eyes up to meet hers. "Better things await me."

The audience goes deathly silent, and I too am mesmerized by his calm. There's a rare beauty about him, one that never graces this stage. Death does not frighten him. How is it he's made his peace with this world and is ready to travel into the next? He looks serene, content even.

Then I blink, and his eyes have rolled back into his head. I don't realize I've grabbed Ryder's hand until she squeezes mine. I've watched a lot of auctions, but Kellen's cries strike me harder than most, like a knife hitting bone.

The Memory Auction has begun.

CHAPTER
2

It doesn't take long for Madame to sort through Kellen Marks' memories. He grinds his teeth as she decides what's of value to auction and what terrible events she'll force Kellen to relive before death claims him. Tears stream down his cheeks as he cries out for his mother. His words are strangled and jumbled, but it's clear enough Madame has trapped Kellen in the moment when his mother died. His brow twists before he rears up from the chair, fighting against the chains so hard that the cuffs of his shirt are soaked with blood.

Ryder covers her ears and nestles into me.

My chest burns as I watch him gasp. It only takes a few carefully extracted memories to ensure he can't remember how to fill his lungs. I close my eyes and draw Ryder closer.

A lady shuffles past us, bumping into my shoulder and mumbling things about being late and missing all the good merchandise.

Ryder sticks her foot out, but I jerk her back before the lady trips over it.

"Don't make a scene. Too many Minders," I whisper.

"Not making a scene is what led to this," she mutters, pointing at the stage.

I want to agree with her, but as I clutch Ryder's tiny hand and picture my mother asleep in her asylum bed, my words dry up to nothing.

Kellen's twitching and still struggling to breathe when Madame steps in front of him. "Kellen Marks has paid the price for his acts of treason, and we will judge him no longer. He will now be given the chance to give back to society." She pauses. "He is a fisherman from the city of Blare."

A murmur passes over the crowd and hearing the name of the city where I grew up is like a slap in the face. Though I don't recognize Kellen, fury rushes up inside me as the audience cheers and claps. Bile rises up my throat as I feel their hunger, their unquenchable thirst for whatever joys that Kellen's memories hold.

Blare isn't known strictly for its rickety wharves and seaside cottages. It's the capital of the Coastal Realm where painting, drawing, singing, and dancing are all taught. If Kellen grew up there, he'll be full of artsy talents.

"He was paired and has one child," Madame continues.

28

Hands shoot high in the air as the bidding begins. True love is always a top seller.

On my tiptoes, I catch sight of a bidder and nudge Ryder. "He's from Aravid." As a person's fashion tends to lean toward their most recent memories, whether purchased or created, his thick wool jacket is a dead giveaway he's come from the capital of the Woodland Realm.

Ryder's eyes go wide. "Haven't seen someone from there in months."

Aravid isn't more than a two days' hike from here, but it's the danger of traveling through the common lands between each Realm that discourages most from leaving one of the well-protected capital cities. Ever since Madame came into power after her father was murdered, the woods have been filled with criminals and vagabonds because she pulled all the Minders patrolling the forest back to Craewick.

Some say she did this to protect her people after her father's death. The rarity of a ruler being killed, and the fact that his killer was never found, frightened the Hollows so much that most didn't question Madame's orders. Others argue she did it to drive up the price of auction bids. Because nowadays, unless a person can afford to hire a Minder as an escort, the only hope of gaining new memories is up on that auction block.

Casting a look down, Madame motions for a few Minders to escort the bidder up on stage. Aravid memories are scarce in Craewick, and it's unlikely he'll be outbid. They speak in low tones, quickly deciding which of his memories she'll accept as payment. They've only minutes until Kellen will die, his veins cooling and his pupils fading to white, to retrieve his memories.

As Madame is a Sifter, one whose rare and powerful Gift works through sight and not touch like the rest of the Gifted, the only clue that Kellen's past has moved into this bidder's mind is when Kellen slumps in the chair.

I let out a long breath, relieved he didn't suffer as long as some.

The ecstatic bidder leaves the stage, but it's only a matter of time before he'll sell those memories in search of a grander high.

"He's even walking like Kellen Marks now," Ry murmurs, and I follow her gaze, frowning when I see she's right. The Aravid man is no longer hunched over but standing tall and erect, like Kellen did only minutes ago. "Bet by tomorrow, he'll be rid of that stuffy wool jacket and be dressed like he's from Blare too. Just like you."

"At least my memories of Blare are real," I snap.

She barks out a laugh. "Try telling that Aravid Hollow that his memories aren't real."

A memory from the first auction I ever attended floods back to me.

"Why do you say most of the Gifted are hollow?" I ask Greer.
"Because there's nothing left inside of them."

I frown. How could he say these people were empty when they were stuffed full of rare talents and thrilling memories? "But there's so much inside of them!"

He touches his heart. *"No, nothing left of them, of who they once were . . . they've lost themselves to become someone else."*

The wind picks up, stinging my cheeks. I cross my arms under my cloak, but I can't stop shivering.

The crowd is getting antsy between auctions, but Madame knows how to keep the calm with a talent show.

Standing in front of the prisoners is a whole new crop of Collectors, those who work for the Craewick Treasury and spend years mastering talents throughout the Four Realms. It's not a terrible career, I guess, traveling from one Realm to the next until their minds are a goldmine of talents and experiences. But after they sell those memories tonight, they won't remember any of it. Years of their lives gone in a matter of seconds.

The first offering is from a master of etiquette, which a mother with four feisty children immediately scoops up. As soon as the memories are transferred, she breathes a sigh of relief as her well-mannered offspring follow her obediently off the stage.

Next, a cliff-jumper whose leg is bound by a bloodied cloth hobbles onto the auction block. He has this smug look on his face as multiple bidders raise their hands. People will pay a fortune to experience the rush of adrenaline housed deep inside his memories, but cliff-jumpers rarely live long enough to have much of a career. After selling his memories tonight, he won't remember what nearly killed him. He'll climb bigger mountains and jump off taller bluffs until his luck finally runs out.

To close out the show, a couple waltzes to the tune of a woman belting out an aria, but my guess is no one will buy either one of the talents. It's still early. It will take a few more prisoners' auctions—and a few more pints of ale—before the bids flow more easily.

"And here come the orphans," Ry says. "They'll be working late tonight. This crowd's huge."

To our left, kids in threadbare clothes barrel through the less-than-amused audience. Most Ungifted orphans are forced to make a living this way, offering up their minds to store the Hollows' unwanted memories.

I watch a woman hand over a few coins to a tiny boy, gold that won't buy more than a measly meal. She removes her gloves and as they clasp hands, and I wonder what kind of painful memories she'll transfer into him so she can forget about them. A toothache? A nightmare? Memories from a bad relationship?

My heart aches at the sight of the orphan's flushed face, at how the whites of his eyes are yellowing, a sure sign his mind is being overloaded by foreign memories.

"I wish I could get them off the streets too," I tell her, stealing a glance at the stage where Madame is about to start the next bid.

"Well, you saved one orphan."

I swing my arm around her. "Only because she followed me around like a lost puppy after we met."

Ryder snorts. "Probably because you welcomed her into your life with open arms."

That makes me grin. Goodness knows I tried to shove the responsibility of taking care of her onto my neighbors. But once Ry made up her mind that we should stick together, there was no dodging her.

As Madame calls the name of another prisoner, someone pushes us aside before scurrying off toward the stage.

Ry stumbles, but I grab her arm before she falls, the tiny jolts of energy in her Gifted skin tingling beneath my fingertips.

Colors flash behind my eyelids. Fiery warmth coils in my belly as the memory on the tip of her consciousness seeps into my brain. It's a rush, giving into the deep yearning where my Gift begs to be used. But as soon as I realize I've read her mind, I let go of her wrist.

One word pulses through my head, a fragment of a memory that I've accidentally stolen from her.

Shadows.

It's a moment before Ryder clutches her head, her eyes wide as she stares at me. There's always a slight delay between losing memories and the headache the Gifted feel, the sweet spot any thief uses to escape before a victim realizes a memory is missing.

"What did you take?" she asks between breaths.

My knees threaten to buckle as I lean closer, lowering my voice to a raspy whisper. "Why were you thinking about the Shadows?"

She doesn't back down. "Because I'm going to ask them to save your mother."

I gasp. "You *what*?"

Ryder bites her lip as she meets my eyes, her brown curls a nest of tangled strands in the moonlight. "That's what the Shadows do. They help people who can't help themselves."

"Except they haven't been seen in years. They're just a myth now," I whisper harshly.

"Not true." Her eyes dart all around us, but nobody's paying attention to our conversation. They're too enthralled watching the Minders secure a thrashing prisoner to the chair. "I met a Shadow, and I've been waiting for the right time to tell you. I'll ask him to help your mother."

I close my eyes as a cold sweat slithers down my spine. Help her? I want to laugh. To Ryder, I'm a daughter whose comatose mother could use all the help she can get. Not the memory thief who backstabbed the Shadows to pay for that asylum bed in the first place. Surely, Bray, the leader of the underground memory market, wants to do one thing with me—slit my throat. And now four years of hiding could vanish with a single word from Ryder.

"I want *nothing* to do with the Shadows," I hiss. "And if you have any sense, you'll stay away from them too." I back away from her and glance around, searching for signs they may already be watching and waiting to haul me back to Bray. And if they are, I don't want Ryder anywhere near me.

"Don't you want more than this, Etta?" she calls out after me.

Keeping my back toward her, I stop walking. Of course I want more than a life of worrying that Ryder will one day end up on the auction block and watching my mother wither away in the asylum, but I'm not sure I deserve it. Not after everything I've done.

I glance down at the four leather bands on my wrist before I shove my hands into my pockets and push out of the crowd. There's a collective hush in anticipation of the next auction, and I gulp in a breath so I don't scream. The only place I need to be is at the asylum, so that's where I'll head to find a way out of this mess.

Making my way to the edge of the audience, I pull my mother's lottery ticket from my pocket. In the moonlight, a few of the words shine through the envelope.

My heartbeat rushes to my ears as I rip it open. This is no lottery ticket.

It's my mother's Notice of Auction.

CHAPTER

3

On my seventh birthday, I nearly drowned.

The rain had been falling in sheets for days, and white foam capped the waves off the coast of Blare. My mother had been teaching art classes from dawn till dusk, and I was bored out of my mind. So I skipped down to the beach and dove into the frigid water before anyone could stop me.

Waves swept me along the cove, smashing me against the rocky edge until a pair of strong hands lifted me out of the water. I don't remember much of the fisherman who saved me, or the hours my mother bounced between fits of fury that I'd run off and thankful kisses that I was safe.

What I do remember is how it felt to hit that boulder. Like every inch of me shattered into a million pieces. I didn't think there was a more painful feeling, but there is.

The auction notice trembles in my hands. Madame doesn't auction asylum patients! It's a torturous death reserved for thieves and rebels. But my mother has never been either.

That was me.

I lean against the alley wall as my knees give out. What if this isn't a mistake? Auctioning my mother would be far worse than anything Madame could ever do to me. If this had been a lottery ticket, her death would've been painless, not agonizing like up on the auction block.

Now strangers will be given the chance to own her entire life and part of mine, as well. They can buy the memories of me growing up on the beaches of Blare, of my mother teaching me how to paint and draw. And once those memories are gone, scattered among the highest bidders, it'll be as if my mother never existed.

I take off toward the asylum.

This section of Craewick is a maze of alleys, full of beggars and drifters, but the sight of the asylum is what really makes me quiver. From its place high on the hill, it casts a long shadow over the street below as I run up the stone steps. There's always a Minder stationed outside the door to ward off thieves who'd steal from addicts and coma patients, though what's inside is far more frightening than him.

As I push through the doors, frenzied screams fill

the air. The stench of sweat, urine, and blood sparks memories of uneasiness, disgust, and fear.

An addict lunges at me as I pass her. Like everyone else trapped in these rows of cast-iron beds, she's held back by a crisscrossing of chains on her wrists and ankles. Spit trickles from her cracked lips. Scabs dot her hairline where she's torn the hair from her scalp. Housing too many foreign memories has rotted her mind, turned her pupils the color of a raincloud.

We might call the ability to swap memories a gift, but there's only so much energy the mind can handle before it implodes.

Eventually, most addicts will fall into a coma, and their families usually end up selling all the addict's memories to pay for Madame's steep asylum fees. But as these deaths ensure the Craewick Treasury stays well-stocked, it's no wonder why many fail to recover.

I take the stairs to the second floor, where the silence is just as unnerving.

The patients up here rarely move, but their eyes are wide-open, shifting back and forth. Choosing to live in a memory is a common temptation for the Gifted. I never understood giving up reality to live in a fantasy before my mother fell into her coma, but after that, I stopped judging them. It takes a whole lot of pain to make someone want to escape to the past, and most never come back to the present. Memories are a tricky captor.

The man in the bed next to my mother's draws in a shuddering breath. His brow twists as his eyelids flutter open and closed.

I gently pat his shoulder as I pass, though I don't think he understands much. No one's come to visit the whole time he's been here. But it's easy enough to include him when I tell my mother stories, or to make sure he's not getting bedsores and feed him tiny spoonsful of gruel. The nurses call him Baldwin, or bald one, I can't tell which. What I do know is every morning, he wakes with cold feet and his lips curl into a smile when I wrap a blanket around them.

My mother is as still as a corpse under a white sheet. The moonlight creeping in from the floor-to-ceiling window makes her look even paler, ghostly in a way. I used to think having a view was a good thing, but once I realized it perfectly overlooks the auction block, I saw it for what it really was: Madame's less-than-subtle warning to behave.

Tonight's auction is far from over, so I draw the curtain before I turn toward my mother, half expecting her to open her eyes and greet me. It's been four years since I've heard her voice, only days after I turned thirteen.

We're opposites in many ways, except for our tiny statures, white-blonde hair, and hazel eyes. My mother used to say that I was her mirror. The older I grew, the more I saw it too. Though as a child, I caught whispers

about my mother's gentle and loving spirit. Our similarities ended there. So everyone knew where I must've
inherited the inky spots of my nature.

As I do every day, I kiss my mother's cheek and
remind her how much I love her.

There's a cold bowl of gruel on her bedside table, now
too thick to slide down the tube the nurses stick down her
throat to feed her. I curse them under my breath for not
feeding her earlier. My mother is skin and bones already,
but they've never cared for her like they should. None of
them expected her to hold out this long.

"Most coma patients don't live more than a few months," a
nurse told me just after my mother was placed in this bed.
*"Her memories are like the threads of a tapestry but tangled and
woven together in all the wrong places. It makes it very difficult
for her to wake. At least if she dies, you can keep her memories."*

I shuddered at that. I've never wanted my mother's
memories. I've only wanted to make new ones with her.
But the first night at the asylum, I did read my mother's
mind, hoping she could hear me when I spoke and feel
when I touched her hand.

A rush of colors broke forth but none of the memories
made sense. There were gardens in bloom and glittering
fountains, of skies flooded with soft clouds and a tangerine sun. I saw nothing of our home in Blare . . . and no
memories of me.

Not wanting to risk my mother's healing, I didn't

read her mind after that. Only she'll be able to tell me where she's been these past four years, locked in the deep recesses of her mind. That is, if she's given the chance. Because whatever twisted plan Madame has in store for me, Gwendolyn Lark waking up isn't part of it.

I close my eyes as my memories take me back to the day Madame and I struck our deal . . .

Standing in front of the window overlooking the auction block, Madame studies my mother with a look of disgust on her face. "As you have upheld your end of our bargain, Julietta, I shall uphold mine. Your mother will have a place here until she wakes or dies."

I reach down and clutch my mother's hand, staring at the tattoo on my wrist. The swollen, stinging mound of flesh that was free of ink hours ago. My mother and I are both Craewick citizens now, under Madame's watchful eye.

"What are you going to do with Greer?" I force out.

"Exactly what he deserves. He'll be punished and killed," she replies, and my stomach lurches as I imagine the look on his face when he realizes I'm the reason he's in shackles, that I told Madame his location to buy my mother an asylum bed. "The Shadows are more than just a thorn in my side. Crime has increased throughout the Four Realms, compromising the safety of each citizen, and all for what? For Greer to grow rich?"

"It's not about riches," I say through gritted teeth.

"Is that what he tells you? Greer started the black market. He trained you to steal memories from my citizens."

"I only stole what never belonged to your citizens in the first place and gave the memories back to their rightful owners. It's your job to protect the Ungifted, but if you won't, then the Shadows will. They make sure everyone isn't forced to bow down to you," I say.

The corner of her mouth twitches, fury flickers across her face, before she regroups with a tight pull on the hem of her military jacket. *"You are a thief. And a society is only as strong as the morality—"*

I wave her off. *"Yeah, yeah. I've heard your auction speech."*

"But apparently, you weren't listening. You yourself have proven that if one presses on the tiniest crack, the glass will shatter."

"I didn't realize Craewick was so fragile," I say.

"Oh, I'm not referring to Craewick," she says with a pointed look at me, then my mother.

I lose the nerve to tell her it's only under poor leadership that a black market flourishes. We stole from the wealthy to give back to the poor. While the Hollows crowd their minds with foreign memories, the Ungifted live in fear on the fray of Craewick and in the other cities, often victims of theft and forced to sell their own memories just to make ends meet. But Shadows do far more than protect the Ungifted. They're the only family many orphans have ever known, and a safe haven for those on Madame's hit list.

"My rules are strict but designed for the common good," she says.

Ignoring her, I refuse to debate ethics with someone who puts people up for auction. It's a demeaning and painful death, a torturous punishment for whomever she considers a criminal. With all the rules and regulations of Craewick, it's as if Madame sets her people up to fail, then punishes them when they do. She's made herself judge, jury, and executioner.

Madame rests her chin on her bony hand. "My father's rule of Craewick was strict, as well, but there were flaws. Do you know what I vowed the night of his murder?"

I meet her eyes. "That you would hunt down the one who killed him."

She gives a slight shake of her head. "That I would never let the same thing happen to me. Weakness is perceiving a threat and doing nothing to stop it," she says before lifting her wrist to show me her tattoo. It's shaped like an eye, signifying a Sifter's Gift. "Do you know how a Sifter reads minds, Julietta? When I look at a person, their thoughts become my thoughts. It was exhausting at first, hearing all those voices that I couldn't tune out. I heard what people truly thought of me, who they wanted me to be. But as I grew, I learned how to control my Gift and use it only when I wished, listening to myself instead of the thousands crying to be heard."

I've heard this about Sifters, how they struggle to find their own voice. Then there's the temptation to steal whatever they please. Their minds don't fill up as quickly as ours do, their Gifts allowing them to hold much larger amounts of foreign memories. That's why we call them Sifters in the first place. They sift through memories faster than anyone. They can snatch every memory from your brain, and you wouldn't even know who did it before dropping dead.

"When I look at you, however, all is silent," Madame adds.

I lift my chin, trying to appear stronger than I feel, but her grin only widens. I don't know what happened to my mind at the time of my mother's accident, but I'm different now. "The Minders said I was unreadable."

"And so you are. I cannot read another Sifter unless they put their guard down. The energy in our minds creates a barrier to protect us from one another, but you are not like us." She points to the gold flecks in her dark eyes, a trait all Sifters share that I don't. "Your uniqueness is fascinating, though I've seen variations of Gifts before. They are uncommon but not unheard of. You might believe that the fact your mind cannot be read makes you invincible, but you would not have begged for that Ungifted tattoo if you didn't fear for your life."

I glance at my wrist. My Ungifted tattoo is part of the deal we made. After betraying the Shadows, my ability to hide among the masses is the only hope I have that they won't find me. Now I'll live in the fray, among the farmers, seamstresses, and locksmiths, where the Shadows will never think to search for a girl who was once a memory thief.

Madame studies my mother's still body. "This is all your fault, isn't it, Julietta? She is in this coma because you are a liar and traitor . . . Let me see if I understand what really happened in Blare. You implanted dozens of violent memories while attacking who you thought to be a Minder, only to discover it was your *own mother. Didn't Greer teach you to look before leaping into a mind?" Her laugh cuts through me. "You were clever to use your Gift as a weapon, but the Ungifted are a delicate species. One spark of Gifted energy and they burst into flames."*

Her words turn my blood to ice. It all happened so fast. One minute, Minders were swarming my mother and dragging me to face trial for joining the Shadows. The next, my mother crumbled to the floor, her memories fragmented and tangled because I'd mistaken her for an enemy.

"You bought your mother's life with Greer's blood. Now the question you'll ask for the rest of your life is this . . ." Madame meets my eyes. "Was it worth it?"

As the memory drifts away, I clutch my mother's hand. The only movement of her body is the rising and falling of her chest and the brief flutter behind her eyelids. Then her finger twitches. I gasp and draw closer as she taps my hand three times, in the exact same way as when I was a child.

I . . . love . . . you.

A sob catches in my throat. Her fingers are now still, but she's said more than enough before the coma takes her once again. She's coming back to me.

Pounding my fist on my forehead, I sink into the chair. What other option is there but to escape Craewick? Maybe between Ry and me, we could figure out a way to carry my mother . . .

The Shadows can help her.

I brush the memory of Ryder's plan away as another replaces it.

They help people who can't help themselves.

There has to be another solution, but all I can think about is the one person who's powerful enough to slip in and out of the asylum, get my mother out of Craewick, and keep us hidden: Bray, the Sifter whom Greer trained to be his successor.

Sighing, I rub my eyes. How bad have things gotten that I'd even consider contacting my former mentor? Striking deals with my enemies has been disastrous so far, but the black market is nothing like Craewick. There's a use for my unreadability, a skill that could have endless benefits for the Shadows. I'll be the first to admit I don't own many talents, but theft has always come naturally. If I pledged my life to serve Bray, would that be enough to get my mother out of Craewick?

I kiss my mother's cheek, whispering promises that I'll always protect her, before I run out of the asylum.

The crowd surrounding the stage has grown even larger as I push my way toward Ryder, still standing where I left her. "I want to meet with the Shadows," I whisper. "How do I find them?"

Her eyes light up. "I knew you'd change your mind. I'll bring the Shadows to you."

"No, I don't want you getting involved," I practically spit out.

She backs away. "I'm already involved, Etta. Just go home. We'll meet you there."

When I charge after Ryder, a Minder grabs my elbow and yanks me back, his grip as strong as steel as I try to wrench free. "Slow down," he orders, glancing around as a few Hollows narrow their sights on me.

Some shove their hands into their pockets while others pull their collars up to their ears, looking at me like the insurgent I once was. Auctions are like a pile of kindling just waiting for a spark. Once this crowd grows restless, it only takes one scream, only a ripple of suspicion that a thief is among the crowd, to set the whole thing ablaze.

"Let me pass," I say to the Minder, though I've already lost sight of Ry. She's vanished, no doubt using all the tricks I taught her to disappear.

The Minder waits a second longer, as if expecting someone to rush up and accuse me of theft, but he lets me go once Madame starts the next bid.

Stumbling away, I curse myself for dragging Ryder into all this. Now Bray will find out she's my friend. And if he hurts Ry to get back at me for betraying the Shadows, I'll never forgive myself.

My sides split with pain as I sprint to my cottage.

For years I've dreaded the moment when I'd be forced to face Bray. Ever since I betrayed the Shadows, it feels as if his eyes have never stopped watching me. Whenever the wind rattles the lock on my door, I always wonder if he's finally found me. Sometimes I'm just so tired of worrying, so tired of hiding, and so tired of feeling guilty that I almost wish he would.

But now, it isn't just the thought of pledging to Bray which frightens me. It's always a risk to play with memories, when you can't help but sink into a sea of others' wishes, hopes, and dreams . . . but if losing myself means saving my mother, isn't it worth it?

The fray is completely deserted as I up my pace and come out of the alley near my cottage. I throw the door open and lean against it to catch my breath.

Not a second later, a dark hood slips over my head and a deep voice whispers near my ear, "Welcome back to the Shadows."

CHAPTER

4

Many nights when I was young, I'd wake up crying from the nightmares that trouble Gifted children.

My mother would crawl into bed beside me, doing her best to explain that fear sits on the tip of our consciousness, and burying heartbreak and pain proves an impossible task for most people. Whenever I touched someone, I'd accidentally steal what most were trying hard to forget. Those dark, chilling memories haunted my dreams. My mother would rest her chin on top of my head as I nestled close. Her voice was soft and sweet as she lightly sang snippets of the Realms' Songs.

The memory of my mother, of how safe I felt pressed against her, provide a few seconds of comfort before my mind snaps back to reality.

I pull my knees up to my chest and rock back and forth. The stone floor is icy and damp, and I haven't stopped shivering since I woke up here.

I'm in the Mines now, where the best thieves in the Realms live, trade, and vanish right out from under Madame's watchful eye. It's a safe haven, a black market of memories, and a fortress so well protected that the Minders have never been able to find it. Any memories you want, from rare talents to secrets the Shadows use for blackmail, you'll find far below the Realms in this underground city.

And to be back here, not as a thief but as a captive, fills me with dread.

The walls aren't thick enough to block out the screams of the other prisoners, trapped in pitch-black cells like mine. I cover my ears as their cries pierce the silence.

Greer used these dungeons to lock up Minders who got too close to the Mines. He'd read their minds, erasing any memories which could lead Madame to our base, then set them free. He wasn't violent unless forced to protect one of his Shadows, often showing mercy to those who didn't deserve it.

Judging from the sound of those screams, Bray has taken a different approach to dealing with enemies.

My stomach twists at the sharp, cloying scent of dried blood clinging to every inch of the cell. I pinch the bridge of my nose, willing myself not to get sick. The darkness plays with my mind. Snippets of memories flash behind my eyelids.

Cade and Joss, two of my Shadow partners, appear before me. I miss them so much my heart feels as if it'll split in two, but it isn't until I see Penn's face that I bite back a sob. I touch the four leather bands on my wrist, three of which once belonged to them.

Breaking free of the memories, I open my eyes and hit the wall with my fist, furious at myself for ever believing Bray would help me. Every passing second draws my mother closer to Auction Day. For four years, she's battled her coma, far surpassing any expectations placed upon her. She hasn't given up. I can't fail her now, not when she's so close to waking.

I push myself to my feet and scream, pounding on the door. If fighting my way back to my mother means escaping the Shadows, I'll do it or die trying. My hands are bloody and bruised when someone finally comes.

As soon as I see who's standing in the doorway, I recoil to the corner of my cell.

Gone are his boyish looks, his features sharp and refined now, as Bray towers over me. My legs threaten to give out as he studies my face. I will myself not to look away as his eyes meet mine. My mind is unreadable now, but if this surprises him, his expression reveals nothing. I'm still positive he's wishing he could make my heart forget to beat.

He shuts the door and sets his lantern on the floor. "You're supposed to be dead, Jules."

Deep, bitter rage rolls off him, but the lightness of his tone sends a shudder down my spine just before he lunges at me. Bray slams me against the wall and wraps his hands around my neck.

"For years, I thought Madame had murdered you. But just before I killed the Minder who slit my brother's throat, that coward told me you were the one who betrayed Greer," Bray whispers near my ear. "Ever since then, do you know how many times I've wished for this moment?"

I claw at his hands as he tightens his grasp. Black spots crowd my vision. My lungs feel as if they're on fire. "I had no idea Cade and Joss were with him," I rasp. "Madame was going to murder my mother if I didn't give up Greer's location!"

Clenching his jaw, Bray lets me go, and I crumble at his feet.

"I wish I'd died that day instead of them," I whisper.

He crouches down in front of me, and I back away, pressing against the wall. "Finally, something we agree on," he says, calm and in control once again as he slips my mother's auction notice of out his pocket and holds it up. "I had no clue either one of you was still alive until your little friend Ryder came begging for our help last night—"

"Where is she?" I shout. "Don't hurt her."

Bray's eyes flash. "Why would I hurt the person who brought you back to me? She's proven herself to be more valuable than I ever thought possible. She'll make an excellent Shadow while you're finally getting what you deserve."

"I'm begging you, Bray, leave Ryder out of this. And don't let Madame kill my mother! She's innocent," I cry.

"Your betrayal is what will kill your mother. You'll be her murderer, not Madame."

His words cut through me as he drops the notice on the floor.

"Get my mother out of Craewick, and I'll do whatever you want—"

"There is nothing I want except to see you suffer," he says through his teeth. "Now your mother's death will haunt you as my brother's haunts me. We'll share a similar fate, Jules, never being able to save the people we love. And there is no worse feeling than that."

Panic rises up inside me as he stands and turns toward the door. I stuff the auction notice into my pocket before I push myself to my feet and throw myself in front of him. "Greer would want you to save her. He helped people who couldn't help themselves," I say.

"And look where that got him," Bray hisses. "You're a traitor and a liar, and you'll be treated just like any other prisoner."

"But I'm not like any other prisoner! I can be useful to

you," I yell back, pointing at my head. "I know you see I'm unreadable. I don't know why, but now nobody can break into my mind, not even Sifters." I show him the tattoo on my wrist. "I begged Madame for this Ungifted tattoo so I could hide from you, but it can make me an asset to the Shadows. I can steal any memory, and nobody will ever suspect I'm the thief or be able to take the memories back from me. If you'll get my mother out of Craewick, I'll never question your orders or refuse any job. My life will be yours."

Dread coils in my stomach as his face darkens. In his silence, I shudder as another scream erupts outside my cell. I picture my mother, helpless and alone in her asylum bed. If I don't convince Bray that I'm of any worth to him, that's exactly how she'll remain until Auction Day.

"I promise you that I'll suffer. Being separated from my mother will tear me apart," I whisper. "Just don't let her die."

Bray lifts my chin with his finger, forcing me to meet his stare. The gold flecks in his green eyes look as if they're on fire. "Greer was as much of a father to me as my own. You betrayed him, you betrayed me, and you betrayed my brother. Every time I dream, I see their faces and hear them crying out for help, but no one comes to rescue them. If you betray me again, your fate will be no different."

"I won't betray you," I force out.

"Your words mean nothing to me."

"Then let me prove it! What do you want me to do?"

"Help me kill Madame," he says without hesitating.

A memory of Madame flashes before me. Her eyes are shifty, always calculating, but her voice is as flat as the expressions on her face. She gives off the impression she's not listening, as if her mind is lost somewhere, but always responds with the correct answer. Usually before you've even finished asking the question. She's one step ahead. Always.

"Madame anticipates threats before the plan even hatches," I stammer. "Nobody can kill her."

"You're wrong, Jules," he says. "There is a Sifter more powerful than her. We have the ability to transfer memories, but he has the ability to transfer *Gifts*. He can change a Gifted into an Ungifted. He can strip Madame of her power, and she'll never even see it coming."

My heartbeat rushes to my ears. "Who?"

He pauses, then meets my eyes. "Greer."

I stumble away from him. A thousand memories fly through my head of all the years I spent with Greer. He taught me not only how to read minds but people, how to pinpoint weaknesses and strengths . . . and yet I failed to notice his?

"If that's true, why didn't Greer fight back when the Minders captured him?" I ask as my throat closes. "Why didn't he steal Madame's Gift when he had the chance?"

"Because she used Cade and Joss as leverage until he

was subdued," Bray says, his words clipped. "Greer was a willing prisoner, and Madame killed them anyway. I saw everything in the memories of the Minder who murdered my brother. I even know what happened to Penn."

Hot, angry tears flood my eyes as the memory of his death flashes before me.

Blood seeps from the corner of Penn's mouth and the look in his eyes is louder than any scream.

"But Madame said she killed Greer too," I say.

"Death would've been too quick for someone she hated as much as Greer. Madame sent him to the Maze."

Tears trickle down my face as I squeeze my eyes shut. *The Maze.* It's a prison invented by a madman named Porter, the ironfisted Sifter who rules the Woodland Realm from his fortress in Aravid.

The rumors passed around the Realms say the Maze is a labyrinth of bone-thin prisoners chained to stone walls, whose minds Porter fills with horrific memories that they're forced to relive until they die. Others claim the entire prison is actually a maze of tricks and traps, designed to make the sane go insane.

Though the thought of Greer rotting away in the Maze makes me tremble, the tiniest flame of hope flickers inside me. Madame didn't kill him!

"Greer has been trapped in there for four years," I say, terrified to voice my next question. "How do you know if . . . if he's still . . ."

"Sane? Alive? I don't, but you're going to find out. If anyone could survive the Maze, it would be someone with a Gift as powerful as his."

"But how do you expect me to break in? Nobody knows where it's even located," I say.

Bray raises his eyebrows. "Nobody except the person who designed it. Porter owns the only key to that prison. If you want your mother to live, you're going to steal the map from his mind, break Greer out of the Maze, and bring him back here. Then Greer will take away Madame's Gift and end her reign."

At his words, colors flash before my eyes. I lean over as a memory of Porter threatens to overwhelm me. My stomach quivers as it rushes to the forefront of my mind. I blink, fighting my way back to the present and open my eyes. Greer always kept the Shadows far away from Aravid, claiming Porter wasn't an enemy he wished to make. But one time, I stole a memory of someone who'd met him. The terror she felt in Porter's presence gave me nightmares for weeks.

Porter is a legend, the villain in all of our bedtime stories. Even if this plan works, what about the evil in his thoughts, evil that'll be free to grow inside of me once I take his memories?

I meet Bray's stare. "I can't do this—"

He grabs the collar of my cloak and jerks me off my feet. "What makes you think you have a choice? All it takes is a second to snatch that memory, and with your unreadability, nobody can take it back from you. You will do this, or I'll drag you back to Craewick myself to watch your mother die."

When he lets go, my legs collapse. "You know the energy surrounding a Sifter's mind is too powerful for me to force my way in." I look up at him. "Unless Porter lets me inside his mind first, how am I supposed to steal that memory?"

Bray kneels in front of me. "Give me your hand," he says. When I hesitate, he grabs it anyway. His skin is rough and calloused, but it tingles with the warmth of his Gift as he puts his guard down. "Take only what's on the tip of my consciousness. Try to steal anything from me, and I'll make Madame look merciful."

I close my eyes and let the memory seep into me . . .

From my guard post at the commander's office, I catch snippets of his conversation with Madame. They're yelling about Porter and Aravid. Something about a fire. There's a slit between the hinges, just wide enough to peek in. The commander sits behind his desk, but Madame blocks my view. Something shiny catches my eye, near the corner of the desk as if it's fallen off and been forgotten. I squint . . . a necklace?

"I have ensured these events will never be linked to me or you, Commander," says Madame. "No one will ever know you're the one who told me that Porter's daughter was here."

A bead of sweat trickles down his brow. "How can you guarantee that?"

She lifts a spidery hand in the air. "Memories are easy enough to remove. If nobody remembers what happened, they'll believe she died inside that cottage when it burned to the ground."

"But no one was in that cottage when I torched it," he blurts out. "What if Porter finds her body? The evidence leads straight to us!"

"I am not worried about Porter finding her body." Madame circles the commander like prey.

"Why not?" he spits out. "I most certainly am!"

"Because there is no body," she whispers and slits his throat. "She's still alive."

I came back to the present with a gasp, my head throbbing as my mind adjusts to holding the new memory. "Madame has been lying to Porter?" I say between breaths. "But they're allies!"

His eyes narrow. "Do you really think two brutal rulers wouldn't keep secrets from one another? Anyone who believes they're allies doesn't know a fraction of what's truly going on throughout the Realms."

Bray pulls out a silver chain from beneath his shirt. The pendant is engraved with the crest of the Woodland Realm, the same pattern etched on the clasp of my cloak.

"Porter won't meet with you unless he has a reason to," he says. "Before it was stolen by the Minders, this necklace belonged to his daughter. It'll get his attention, and the memory will prove she's still alive. Offer to give Porter that memory and once you're inside his mind, steal the map of the Maze. It'll disguise your heat signature so he won't know you've taken anything until you're long gone."

My hands tremble as I grab the necklace.

"You said it yourself. Porter will never even see this coming." Bray stares at my Ungifted tattoo before meeting my eyes. "It's ironic, isn't it? Your stupidity gets Greer sent to the Maze, and yet you're the only one who can set him free." He grabs the shoulder of my cloak and drags me to the door. "Before you leave, there's something else you need to see."

Outside the cell, shadows play on the rocky walls. The only light comes from the lanterns strung high above us, though the flames aren't bright enough to do much good. I stumble in the soft dirt and bits of the wall flake off as I graze it. I rub the reddish clay between my fingertips. The tunnel slopes, steep enough that I lean back to keep my footing.

I haven't been here in four years but these tunnels and caverns are so familiar that I could sprint through them with my eyes closed. Though if someone were to ask me *where* the Mines are located, I'd have no clue what to tell them.

Once a thief leaves the safety of this underground fortress, a scout takes the memories of its location and implants a clue on how to find it again: a certain tree deep in the forest. When a thief wishes to return to the Mines, they go to that tree, and the scouts lead them back to a secret entrance. It's one of the protocols to keep the black market hidden.

Because I didn't remember where the Mines were located on the day I betrayed Greer, I believed Madame would never find a way to hurt my friends. I'd never been more wrong.

The tunnel splits into three passageways, and I struggle to keep up with Bray as we take the center one. Ahead, there's a set of wooden stairs built between solid sheets of silver granite. My legs burn as I scramble up the staircase after him. We pass under a rocky arch leading into a massive cavern, where the black market of memories is even grander than I remember.

It's a city built entirely underground, a marketplace of wooden stands and storefronts carved from the granite they once mined throughout these caves before Madame abandoned the shafts to excavate the riches of the mind. The gold veins in the rare stone catch the light from the dozens of fire pits scattered throughout the cave, casting shadows over everything.

There are dozens of thieves around us, some younger than Ryder to those with hair that's entirely white, clasping hands to swap memories. Many have covered their faces with dark masks or scraps of fabric to keep their identities hidden in case the Minders ever search one of their minds. Words like *combat skills* and *dancing talent* are being shouted from atop tiny wooden platforms, the thieves who've stolen those memories looking to trade with another in search of it.

As Bray and I make our way through the crowd, my Gift flares up deep inside me, my skin tingling as I long to use it. It's a feeling I've suppressed for so long, ever since my mother's accident. After what happened to her, after I witnessed just how easily a Gift could destroy an Ungifted mind, the thought of using it made me sick.

But being back here among these thieves lights my skin on fire and gives me strength, filling me up. I've lived among the Ungifted for so long that I've almost forgotten the thrill that comes in using our Gifts to undermine everything Madame stands for. And though I wish more than anything to be the fearless Shadow I once was, I'm terrified that girl died along with Cade, Joss, and Penn.

On the outskirts of the market are stands filled with clothing and thick wool blankets, all items the Ungifted need to cover their skin to protect it from theft and the icy cold of winter. Beside this booth are a few carts filled with fruits and vegetables, items usually given by the Ungifted as a thank you to the Shadows for returning whatever memories they lost.

Bray stops at the edge of the cavern, and I skid to a halt beside him.

Carved into the granite wall are pits filled with fire, where Shadows are melting vats of iron to pour into thick molds shaped like knives, swords, and arrowheads. Others whittle bows from thick branches and loop strings through the notches. They fire the newly crafted arrows across the cavern, hitting painted targets with incredible accuracy.

"The Mines aren't just a den of thieves anymore," Bray tells me. "Greer never wanted to create an army, but that's exactly what we are now. I recruited anyone looking to escape their Minder conscription to fight alongside the Shadows."

I widen my eyes. Like most Sifters, Bray was plucked from his home and sent to the military base in Kripen as soon as the Minders discovered his Gift. I glance at his tattoos, the crest of the Stone Realm above one shaped like an eye. He spent years learning to lead a battalion of soldiers before he escaped to join the Shadows, bringing his brother Cade along after their parents were killed by a drunken Hollow who lost a bid at the auction.

"Greer never created an army because he knew Madame would only destroy it," I say.

"Everyone here is willing to die fighting for what they believe in," Bray answers. "Greer sacrificed everything to keep us safe, but now a future without a revolution is far more frightening than the fight itself. If Greer can't steal Madame's Gift, we're going to burn Craewick to the ground. It'll take a war to draw her out and kill her."

I gasp. "This isn't a fight you can win!"

"It's a risk we have to take. Madame is gaining power, and if you're half the girl you used to be, you'd see it too," he snaps. "Ever since her father was killed, Madame's worst fear is that a more powerful Sifter will take her throne. Her father's advisors always suspected his murder was an inside job—"

"An inside job? So someone he knew?" I ask, and Bray nods. After witnessing how well-protected Madame is, often flanked by Minders or the black-coated hounds which snap at anyone who gets too close, it always struck me as impossible to kill a ruler . . . unless that ruler never saw it coming.

"After his death, Madame became paranoid. She disbanded her father's council and took on all their memories herself. Now she knows every military strategy and way to build an empire. The fact that her mind is capable of holding all that history and not imploding is incredible, but those memories created a thirst for unlimited power. She hates sharing the throne with Porter, Declan, and Sorien, and they don't care much for her either," Bray says.

I nod. The ruler of each Realm is known simply by their surname. Porter of the Woodland Realm, Declan of the Desert Realm, Sorien of the Coastal Realm . . . then you have Madame, who chose not to be associated with her father after she rose to power. Whenever a ruler dies, their throne is taken over by the most powerful Sifter,

66

usually the former ruler's second-in-command, who also hails from that Realm.

Bray adds, "When I lived in Kripen, I noticed Madame visited the military base far more than the other rulers. It took me years of stealing memories off the Minders to figure out why. Madame has been implanting and deleting memories to ensure many of the commanders are loyal to her alone. If my scouts are correct, she's going to attack the other rulers and take control of each Realm a week from today."

"The day after the auction?" I blurt out, my head spinning. I always believed three other Sifters were keeping Madame in line, but if she goes unchecked, how long will it be before the Realms unravel? "But even if their commanders are under some kind of mind control, Porter, Declan, and Sorien will fight her. They won't give up their thrones to Madame."

"They already have. Craewick is the heart of the Four Realms. The Ungifted workers provide food, clothing, and supplies to Blare, Aravid, and Kripen. By controlling who leaves Craewick and what new memories come in, Madame has made herself the lock and key to all its resources. She'll cut off anyone who rises up against her."

"But we've been allied for decades. There have to be people in Craewick who'll fight—"

He barks out a laugh. "Like who? The Hollows? She started the auction to make them willing prisoners, filled up and blinded by foreign memories. They won't bite the hand that feeds them. And the Ungifted aren't equipped for a war like this. How can they protect themselves against Minders, who can erase memories faster than a knife finds its target? The only way to end Madame's reign is to kill her."

I twist my hands by my sides. I've heard conversations like this from my neighbors about life before Madame took her throne just before I was born. When her father ruled, people traveled. They gained new experiences, formed their own identities, and the Ungifted were protected and supported. One of the reasons his death was so shocking is that he was seemingly well-liked among most—so unlike his daughter.

Though I hate Madame as much as my neighbors, I always kept quiet at even the slightest hint of a rebellion. I learned long ago not to encourage their ideas, especially when the discovery of those thoughts will land you an auction slot.

Bray draws closer. "Greer can still prevent this war. If Madame dies, her army will scatter and the Shadows will take over Craewick. You have five days to get the map and break him out of the Maze." He points out a tiny girl with her back toward us. "Don't fail me, Jules. More lives than yours depend on it."

My heart sinks as I watch Ryder nock an arrow and hit a bullseye.

CHAPTER
5

I'll never forget the night I met Ryder.

It was four years ago, just after her grandparents kicked her out of the only home she'd ever known. They'd been selling off happy memories for years to pay rent on their worn cottage until one day, they'd both given away so much of their past that they didn't remember Ryder. She was a stranger to them, an orphan who they wouldn't believe was their own flesh and blood.

I hadn't slept well since my mother fell into her coma, but I'd finally dozed off only to be woken by a little girl sobbing in my doorway, hiding under the tiny overhang as rain pelted down. So I brought her inside and did what my mother had always done to calm me. I wrapped her up in a blanket, warmed some milk, and told her stories until we both couldn't keep our eyes open.

It wasn't until years later that Ryder discovered I'd been keeping secrets from her.

Most don't realize they're Gifted until age ten or eleven, when your skin starts tingling with the energy required to transfer memory, and each time you touch a person, moments you've never lived before seep into your own mind.

Like Ryder had always done, she'd tucked her hand into mine as we walked to the auction, but this time, she reeled back as if I'd set her on fire. "Your skin . . . it's tingling!" she cried.

I'd covered her mouth so quickly I'd frightened her. That's when I knew she was Gifted like me, as only another Gifted could sense the energy in my skin. My fake tattoo had been enough for the Ungifted to accept me as one of their own, and as hardly any Gifted lived in the fray, nobody had ever suspected I was lying. The seamstress had even given me a job sewing Minder uniforms.

Ryder had pushed my hand away. "Why would you pretend to be Ungifted?"

I'd gone deathly still, terrified that Ryder knew my secret but also, I hated that the Minders would soon discover hers.

The Gifted were usually so proud of their Gifts that the second they felt their skin buzz with energy, they rushed to Madame's office to receive their tattoos. Then those from the fray were usually taken from their families and drafted into the Minders or given jobs as Collectors. Unlike the children of the Hollows, whose minds were full of memories and talents passed down from older generations, Ryder had no family and owned nothing of value that she could offer Madame to avoid either career.

I couldn't bring myself to tell her that I'd struck a deal with Madame to get this tattoo. So I lied, saying that I hadn't realized I was Gifted until long after the Minders had already branded me.

"My mother is in a coma because a Gifted destroyed her mind. I want nothing to do with them," I'd whispered, too ashamed to confess I was really the one who'd hurt my mother.

"The Gifted took my grandparents from me too," Ryder said, slipping her hand back in mine. "If you keep my Gift a secret, I'll keep yours a secret too."

We both knew that eventually the Minders would question why she didn't have a tattoo and test her skin for energy. But Ryder was so tiny that we told everyone she was younger than she really was. So far, nobody had questioned her on it.

Brushing the memory away, I spin and shove my hands into Bray's chest, any fear I felt toward him dissolving into fury. "Ryder isn't some soldier in your ill-fated army. Let her go," I say.

"She pledged to me on her own," Bray says. "Ryder is brave enough to stand up to Madame, which is obviously more than I can say for you."

Turning my back toward him, I watch Ryder loose another arrow before I push through the group of Shadows around her and pull Ry into my arms.

"Etta! I knew the Shadows would help you," she cries, dropping her bow to hug me back. "Where's your mother? Is she here?"

"You have to get out of here," I whisper near her ear. "Go to the woods and hide until this is all over."

She jerks away. "Hide? No, I joined up to fight."

I barely stop myself from laughing. What kind of fight would it be? Ryder up against Minders three times her size? "If something happens to you—"

"Who cares what happens to me? This is our chance to change Craewick. We're going to knock Madame off her throne," Ryder says as the glint in her eyes returns. "You protected me from Madame when nobody else would, and now it's my turn to help the rest of the orphans. I can be *their* Etta."

Blinking back tears, I wrap my arms around her again. My mother once told me our friends make up parts of our souls. If that's true, I'm not sure I can afford to lose any- more, but I've never seen Ryder look this way, as if she's finally found her place in the world.

"Did you pledge to Bray?" she asks as I pull back and

nod. She looks over my shoulder and smiles, pointing at something behind me. "Bray's with Reid. He's the one who recruited me."

Narrowing my eyes, I follow her gaze. He's nearly as tall as Bray, and wearing a dark jacket, the same color as the hair clipped close to his head. He isn't wearing any kind of mask, but I don't recognize his face. If I sketched it, I'd draw a lot of edges. He's striking, I'll give him that. He has a chiseled jaw and a bit of a hooked nose, and he angles his head when I catch his eyes. I wonder if he knows about my betrayal. If that's why his stare is so intense.

Ryder grins. "When this is all over, we're going to be a real family, aren't we? You, me, and your mother."

My throat is so tight that I can barely answer. "I'm leaving for a few days, but I'll be back before the fight begins. Be careful, okay?"

She hugs me once more before I force myself to leave her as Bray calls my name. Turning away, I roughly wipe away a tear as it rolls down my cheek. Bray made it clear that my mother's fate is connected to freeing Greer, but the thought that I've also failed to protect Ryder threatens to crush me.

I find Bray near the armory still speaking with this Reid. Recognizing his voice, I hiss, "You're the one who knocked me out and threw me into that dungeon."

Reid blinks twice. "For someone who actually *wanted* to meet with Bray, you put up a pretty good fight."

Bray frowns at me before saying to Reid, "Get your supplies and head out now. Plan to be in Aravid in two days."

Reid glances over. "From what I experienced first-hand, you already own a combat skill, correct? Or should I get you one before we go?"

"We?" I scowl at him, then at Bray. "I don't need a partner."

Bray raises his eyebrows. "The woods between here and Aravid are crawling with Minders, Hunters, and Ghosts. Once Madame realizes one of her precious citizens has escaped Craewick, she'll send soldiers to haul you back, especially if she's auctioning your mother to get back at you. Not to mention Reid will keep you safe in the Maze. Having a Sifter on your side—"

I point at Reid. "You're a *Sifter*?"

Blocking my view of him, Bray puts his hands on his knees so we're face-to-face, making me feel like a child. "He can read ten minds in a second while according to Ryder, you've barely used your Gift in four years. Why is that, hmm? Are you ashamed of being Gifted?" When I don't answer, he adds, "When you come across enemies, do you really think it'll be you or Reid who'll stop them? I won't let your pride ruin this, Jules."

"Etta," I say, matching his sharp tone. "I haven't gone by Jules in years."

Bray looks at me long and hard, and a shudder runs

down my spine. He glances at the four leather bands around my wrist, and I cross my arms to cover them up.

When he finally speaks, his voice is a low growl. "You are alive because you're useful to me. The second that changes, all bets are off." He closes the space between us, and I can't bring myself to meet his stare. "Bring Greer back here before Auction Day, and I'll get your mother out of the asylum. Fail me again, and I'll make you wish you really did die four years ago."

As Bray walks away, I watch him until he's swallowed up by the thieves of the memory market. The back of my throat stings as I blink away tears. Cade, Joss, and Penn do haunt me, but it isn't just them that I mourn. There have been a lot of ugly words between Bray and me, but we share a past, one in which I wouldn't be me apart from knowing him.

Reid is picking through a pile of weapons as I turn toward him. "What's your name?" he asks, without looking up. "Jules? Etta? Which is it?"

"Why do you care?" I mutter.

He holds up a knife with a notched blade and one with a curved handle, glancing between the two. "You seemed to care with Bray."

I shift my feet. My mother always called me Julietta. Greer nicknamed me Jules. In Craewick, I'm Etta. Jules drags up memories of someone I've tried for a long time to forget. "Etta," I tell him.

Reid meets my eyes. "Okay, Etta, why are you looking at me like I'm your enemy?"

"Because you recruited Ryder," I say through clenched teeth. "For four years, I've worked to keep her away from all this and now here she is, giddy at the thought of fighting Minders who'll kill her with one blow. Nobody deserves to be bait to draw Madame out of her lair."

"I agree. That's why I volunteered to go with you to Aravid. I'll do whatever it takes to keep you safe."

"Did you make the same promise to Ryder when you recruited her?" I snap.

Reid clenches his jaw. "Listen, I don't like this plan either. I'd try to steal that map off Porter myself, but I'm not the one who's unreadable." He studies me, the slight glow of the gold flecks in his eyes making me wonder if he's trying to look inside my mind.

At his slight frown, I lift my chin, knowing he failed to read me. "If a Sifter as powerful as Madame can't hear my thoughts, there's no way you or any other Sifter can either."

"That's exactly my point. If I let my guard down to share a memory with Porter, my mind is no longer protected against him. He'll destroy anyone Bray sends except for you. You're the perfect thief."

I throw my hands up. "What if Porter kills me? Will you go to Craewick and get my mother out of the asylum? Will you keep Ryder safe when she goes up against

Minders three times her size?" I spit out. "What happens if we fail?"

His face softens for a brief moment. "The answer to that question scares me as much as it does you. You don't have to trust me, but we both know Bray wouldn't make us partners if he thought I'd hurt you." Leaving the armory, he strides toward the booths on the fringe of the market, saying over his shoulder, "You're stuck with me, Etta. Better get used to it."

He stops at a booth stockpiled with everything we need for the journey to Aravid. There are boxes of matches, compasses, thin blankets, coils of rope, extra clothing, loaves of bread, and bottles filled with water. It's unmanned, these supplies meant for any Shadow to take.

Reid holds up a knife in one hand and an arrow in the other. "What's your specialty?"

When firelight catches the blade, a memory flashes before me.

I've snatched the skill I wanted ever since joining the Shadows—a fighting talent. My veins tingle with satisfying warmth as years of sparring practice dissolve into my every muscle. I've mastered an intricate, lethal dance.

I blink, and the memory fades. "Both. I stole the skills off a Minder."

He looks a little impressed, then hands me the knife and the bow before we rummage through the supplies.

After finding a satchel, I stuff it full with throwing knives, a thin rope, a blanket, matches, and a compass before I place the auction notice on top. I pull a dark tunic over my thin undershirt before securing the clasp of my mother's cloak at my neck. The chain of Porter's daughter's necklace is as cold as ice against my skin.

Reid and I are dressed alike—no bright colors or fancy designs. Plain, simple, and unnoticeable. Like Bray said, the last thing we want is to wake a sleeping beast— the Minders, Hunters, and Ghosts roaming the forest between the Mines and Aravid.

I follow Reid out of the cavern, down dusty tunnels, and up stairways. At the top of one, he opens the latch of a trapdoor and disappears outside.

Taking in a breath, I stare up at the starry sky and put one foot in front of the other, wondering if Greer will be with us when we return. Or if we fail to find the Maze, will Bray be waiting at the end of this tunnel, ready to fulfill his oath to drag me back to Craewick to watch my mother's murder?

But there's one question that haunts me even if this plan goes off without a hitch. If we free Greer from the Maze, what will he say to the girl who betrayed him?

CHAPTER

6

The forest surrounding the Mines is a sea of rich colors glimmering in the starlight. Ruby reds, mossy greens, rusty oranges, and pale yellows. It's such a change from all the gray in Craewick that I spin once to take it in before looking up.

Hidden high in these dense trees are scouts ready to shoot an arrow into anyone they don't recognize, an unfortunate consequence of getting too close to one of the hidden entrances. Normally, we'd transfer our memories of the base into a scout, but as Reid is a Sifter and I'm unreadable, both our minds are protected from anyone we might come across in the woodlands.

Reid swings his pack onto his back and his bow over his shoulder. "We're two days from Aravid. We can't take any breaks and we won't stop hiking until nightfall. We'll rest a few hours then get moving again." He doesn't move, clearly wanting to take up the rear.

"Fine," I say. "I'll keep watch."

"Not a chance."

I lift my chin. "I remember how dangerous it is out here. Worried I've lost all my Shadow senses?"

"Something like that," he replies.

Fastening a knife to my belt, I put my pack over my shoulder. "Don't look so worried, Reid. I'm very good at what I do. Didn't Bray tell you?"

"He did, right before he mentioned you were a liar with a hidden agenda."

I give him my sweetest smile. "Only on my best days."

As we walk, I catch glimpses of my old life with the Shadows. Memories of Cade, Joss, and Penn that I'd buried deep enough to forget, but the calm of these woods rattles them from their hiding place.

Cade darts between the trees, calling for us to keep up. Though Cade's hair was curlier and his green eyes as light as moss without any gold flecks, his face was nearly identical to Bray's.

Beside me, Joss giggles in a way Cade alone makes her do, sweeping her dark braid over her shoulder as she chases after him.

Penn's shoulder brushes against mine, and I turn to smile at him before my friends disappear.

The sound of Reid's voice pulls me from the memories. "This has to be difficult for you."

I angle toward him as I step over a fallen log. "In what way? The fact that my mother is days away from being murdered, or that I just pledged my life to a man who wants to murder me himself?"

"All of it." Reid motions around us. "Shadows spend most of their lives traveling through these woods. Does it bring up a lot of memories?"

I bite my lip. What am I going to tell him? That with every leaf crunching beneath my boots, Cade appears, all gangly legs and boundless energy, running circles around us? That the babbling brook we're passing sounds like Joss's laugh, the funny sound we used to tease her about just to make her giggle more? That every time a bird whistles, high and sharp, I see Penn put his hands to his mouth and match it perfectly?

I think of Baldwin in the asylum, who lives deep inside his mind. The nurses call him imprisoned, but maybe it's better to be imprisoned with people you love than free and alone.

Fiddling with the necklace Bray had given me, I don't answer Reid. Instead, I ask, "You know why I pledged to Bray, but why did you?" I point at his unbranded left wrist. "No tattoo, so the Minders don't know you exist. Why would someone with a Gift as powerful as yours willingly give up his freedom?"

In his silence, my memories flare up, dragging me back to the moment I learned just how terrifying a Sifter's Gift could be . . .

These two Minders can't be much older than me. Both are Gifted, but only one is a Sifter. I can't see his tattoo, but I can tell he has the rare Gift by the row of metals on his uniform, a sure sign he's training to become a commander.

Sifters are prized by the Minders, often rising quickly through the ranks to lead large battalions. Unlike the rest of us, their minds hold so much energy that it serves as a barrier against other Sifters, a guard they can choose to let down whenever they wish to share memories.

Under the sweltering Kripen sun, the boys circle one another on the street like the hounds guarding Madame's mansion.

I hop off the barstool and draw closer to watch them before I glance behind me, where Bray is busy bartering with the tavern's owner. Half of Bray's face is covered by a black rag, his wrist wrapped in the same cloth to hide his tattoos. So far, no one's recognized him as a former soldier who abandoned his post. Greer worries whenever we're here, but the riches of Kripen are too tempting for Bray to stay away.

Because it's a military base, you'd think this city would be full of rules. Instead it's a reeking pit of underground trading and clandestine soldiers, where the Minders are birthed from the mother of the black market.

"Please," the Sifter boy begs his commander. "Don't make us do this."

"Fight," the commander barks.

Both soldiers refuse until the commander drags another soldier forward and cracks a strip of leather across her back. "I can do this all day," he yells. "Let's see how your regiment likes paying for your insubordination."

I recoil, wondering what these soldiers have done to deserve being pegged against one another as they stare each other down.

The Gifted collapses on the dusty street, convulsing like the addicts in the asylum as the Sifter rips every memory from his companion's head. And when he dies, his eyes are wide open and white as snow.

I blink twice, escaping the memory to meet Reid's stare. "Bray must be holding something over you," I say. "Leverage of some kind to keep you bowing before him?"

Reid's smirk is laced with anger. "Seems you've got me all figured out."

"Not at all, but at least I know I'm Bray's prisoner," I say lightly, angling my head. "Do you know you're his prisoner too?"

When he doesn't answer, I turn my back toward him and keep walking.

We hike the rest of the day in silence and make camp long after the sun disappears. It's not a large clearing but inconspicuous, the overlapping treetops forming a roof above us.

Swinging my pack to the ground, I slump down against a thick stump and stretch my legs on a pile of leaves. My stomach growls, my calves are tight, and with every blink, it gets harder to force my eyelids back open.

Reid drops his pack beside me. "I'll make sure we're not being followed."

Shivering, I wrap my cloak tighter around me as he disappears behind the tree line. Every time a branch breaks or a wolf howls in the distance, I jump. I curse myself for being so skittish, though there aren't a lot of things worse than meeting bloodthirsty Ghosts in the dead of night. Reid can sift through a dozen minds in a second, but even he'd have a difficult time against a league of Ghosts.

Shadows are taught to stay anonymous, never engaging in a fight that doesn't involve one of us, but Ghosts are different. In the black market, torturous memories are just as pricy as the pleasant ones, but Greer refused to work with Ghosts. They're in the business of not only selling but creating the memories they use to make a client's enemy suffer.

If you're unlucky enough to meet a Ghost, chances are you'll come away bloody and unable to remember how you got that way after they steal your memories. They're the reason why Shadows work in teams while traveling through these woods, why Bray taught us how to disappear if we were being tracked. All the skills I used to hide from him in Craewick.

Lifting my arm from beneath my cloak, I touch the leather bands on my wrist, three of which belonged to Penn, Cade, and Joss. Madame must've noticed mine and calculated these bracelets meant something to me because she delivered Cade's and Joss's to my cottage after their deaths. She did that for a while, sending gifts that gave me nightmares. Pieces of my mother's jewelry, a lock of Joss's dark hair, a silver ring that belonged to Greer. And finally the Notice of Auction . . . her greatest one yet.

The bands embossed with a *C* and a *J* are darker than Penn's because I never could get the bloodstains out. I run my fingers over the soft leather and trail of black stiches I added because it snapped when I pulled it off Penn's body.

I lift my head at the sound of twigs breaking all around me.

Slowly, I push myself to my feet and slip my knife off my belt, careful to keep it by my side and not make any sudden movements. Sweat slithers down my spine as I count the footsteps. Too many to be Reid. It's almost pitch-black in the clearing, the moonlight barely able to seep through the treetops, but when the back of my neck tingles, I know without a doubt that I'm being watched.

My fighting skill flares up inside me, the warmth of my Gift lighting my skin on fire. But I haven't used this talent in four years. My hands shake as I grip the hilt of my knife. Is Reid right? Has living in Craewick dulled my instincts?

One second, I'm the only one in this clearing. The next, three Minders in gray uniforms are in front of me.

For the tiniest moment, I convince myself it's only a coincidence that we've made camp near theirs until the Minder closest to me says, "Julietta Lark. We've been looking for you."

I blink twice, cursing my mind for playing games as memories of Madame flash before me. He says my name like there's an extra *t* in the middle. There's only one person I've ever heard do that. But she's back in Craewick. Far, far away from here.

Juliettta.

My heartbeat rushes to my ears. It's in the way he angles his head, how his eyes gloss over, that makes this Minder vanish and Madame appear. I see the gold flecks in her dark eyes and the slight clench of her jaw as I back away from him. It's as if I'm staring straight at her.

The leader raises his palms in mock surrender. "We don't want to hurt you."

But we will, is the part he left out. I know how runaways are treated, with their bruised necks and beaten faces. I clench my hands into fists. For four years, I was a willing prisoner of Madame's, but now? The only way I'm getting dragged back to Craewick is black and blue.

I glance at each soldier. One favors his left side, his

weight on that foot and his knife in that hand. The Minder on the right is more balanced, making it harder to read on which side he'll attack first.

The leader grabs my chin, forcing me to meet his stare. His hand trembles and his eyes are cloudy, muddled with whatever memories Madame gave him to help locate me. He's weak, an easier target than he believes himself to be.

"Since you've been gone, Gwendolyn Lark has stopped breathing. Twice." A smile flickers across his face as I call him a liar. "What type of daughter abandons her mother days before her auction?"

Knowing the element of surprise is the only thing on my side, I force myself to remain perfectly still until I lunge at him. I dig my feet into the soft dirt, using his own weight against him as we crash into a tree. It knocks the wind out of him. I revel at the shock on his face as I punch his throat and stoop low before he can hit mine.

The Minder on the left attacks first, as predicted, on my right side. I duck under his reach and punch his kidney before shoving the heel of my hand into his nose.

Blood spews down his face as someone grips my arm and wrenches it backwards. The third Minder. Pain sears through my shoulder, but I refuse to drop my knife. I kick his knee as hard as I can. A scream bellows out behind me as he lets go.

I dart toward my pack, going for my other knives, as my legs fly out from under me. My forehead slams against something sharp. An image of Madame flashes before me as the Minder leader whips me around and pins me to the ground. He hits my wrist against a rock, forcing me to drop my knife. I cry out as his forearm bears down on my collarbone, and the chain of the necklace buries deep into my skin.

"We have orders to keep you alive, but it doesn't matter what condition you're in when we drag you back to Craewick," he hisses. "Fight us all you want. No one's coming to help you."

I claw at his arms, his Gifted skin tingling beneath mine. I close my eyes and leap into his mind, searching for memories I can use as leverage against him.

Images flash behind my eyelids, passing so quickly I feel dizzy as the Minder shuffles his thoughts, clearly sensing I'm inside his head. I don't let go of his arm, even as he tries to wrench it away. Thinking of those I'd die to protect, I shift to that part of his brain too.

Minds can only keep so much hidden, categorized by importance and emotion. One of his most precious memories—the first time he held his son—is right where I imagined. Unprotected and unsuspecting.

Just waiting for a thief.

Before I latch on, the Minder backhands me so hard across the face that I'm forced to pull out of his mind. Hot, furious anger surges inside me. I bring my hands up and shove his elbows down, then plant my feet on the ground and raise my hips. The resistance is enough to get him off balance. When he wobbles forward, I twist my body, shove him off, and reach for my knife.

But just before I plunge the blade into his back, the Minder's face goes blank and his knees buckle before he collapses. The other two soldiers are already unconscious, the shackles meant for me in a heap beside them.

When Reid strides into the clearing, I'm relieved, then jealous that he's knocked out three Minders without laying a hand on them.

We take off immediately and without speaking, knowing we've only minutes before these Minders will wake.

Darting between the trees, I grit my teeth as we jump over fallen logs and duck under gnarled branches. Blood trickles down my face, the cut from the Minder's hit feeling as if it's on fire. I struggle to keep up with Reid's quick, nearly effortless stride. He's careful to keep me within sight, and irritation ripples through me each time his eyes meet mine. I hear myself telling Bray that I don't need a partner and bristle at the fact that Reid has already proved me wrong.

When we come to a rushing stream, we wade into the water to cover our tracks.

"We need to dress that cut before you lose too much blood," Reid says.

"What we *need* is to put more distance between those

Minders and us," I say between breaths, checking to make sure the necklace is still around my neck. "I can keep going."

Clutching my elbow, Reid yanks me out of the stream onto a mossy bank, forcing me to sit on a fallen log as he digs in his pack, pulls out a rag, and dips it into the water. He brushes the hair that's come out of my braid away from my face and presses the cool cloth over the cut.

Tears sting my eyes as I take over for him.

"I shouldn't have left you," Reid murmurs.

"It . . . wasn't . . ." I swallow hard as I bear down to staunch the bleeding. ". . . your fault."

"That's not what I meant," he snaps, and I meet his stare. "We're partners, remember? You didn't even try to get my attention. You just decided to fight them off on your own." He points at my cut. "And look how well that worked out for you."

"Don't you dare get angry at me," I hiss. "What did you expect me to do after they blindsided me? Not put up a fight until you got back? If this is about your pride—"

"This isn't about my pride, Etta! This is about keeping you alive and the fact that your pride, not mine, is going to get you killed." He snatches a bottle from my pack and mutters, "I'll get you some water."

I clench my jaw as I watch him, his words churning over in my mind like the tiny rapids in the stream. How dare he judge me for defending myself. If given the choice, I'd fight those Minders all over again, and I'm just about to tell him that when I bite my tongue. I can't deny that he's awakened something inside me that's deeper than anger, something I've longed for ever since betraying the Shadows. Greer had this saying . . . *"If you want to work alone, if you don't want to answer to anyone, then you're not a Shadow. We depend on one another. We make each other better. Stronger. One is none when two are one."*

Though I don't trust Reid, being able to depend on someone is a feeling I've missed more than I care to admit.

He hands me the bottle filled with ice-cold water, and I press it against my face to numb the pain. I eat a cracker, hoping food might help settle my nerves though my appetite is long gone. Each time I blink, an image of those Minders appears and with it, memories of Madame. I can't get what they said about my mother out of my head. Has she really stopped breathing?

Reid sits against a log across from me and bites into an apple.

I squint at the shadows behind him, but it's too dark to see if anyone's lurking.

"Those Minders won't track someone they don't remember," he tells me.

"Well, that's a helpful trick." And because that comes out sounding sarcastic, I add, "I don't regret fighting those Minders, but I understand your Gift . . . has its uses."

He raises his eyebrows and takes another slow bite.

I sigh. "Fine. I'm thankful for what you did back there."

"Madame might be searching for you, but she hasn't anticipated me. We'd be stupid not to use that to our advantage." He pauses, tossing the apple core into the woods. "I'm pretty impressed with you though."

I pour more water onto the rag before placing it back on my cheek. "Impressed with what? My humble apology?"

This earns a slight smile. "By the way you fought. I can tell you stole that skill from a soldier. Your lines are clean, your moves precise. You were holding your own against three Minders. Turns out you're quite an ally."

"Just not the ally you want," I cut in, unable to remember a conversation between us that hasn't ended in an argument.

"Don't put words in my mouth. You're exactly the one I want."

"What was it you called me this morning? A liar with a hidden agenda?" I ask.

"Bray called you that, not me."

I let out a laugh. "So if you could choose any other Shadow to be your partner, you'd still want me? Forgive me if I don't believe that."

"Believe what you want, but it's true. People always say being a Sifter is the greatest Gift, but do you know how long it's been since I had a partner who I didn't have to worry about accidentally reading their mind?" he asks.

"But you can control your Gift, right? You're not reading everyone you're looking at," I say.

"Sure, like how you don't steal memories every time you touch someone. But still, it only takes a second of my Gift flaring up to learn more than I should. Most people deserve to keep their secrets."

I study him. "Well, I've never heard a Sifter talk like you, but I guess it's not always a gift to know what someone thinks of you."

"Some people make that abundantly clear without having to read their thoughts."

This time, I meet his grin.

"But really, Etta, it's a relief to be around you. Not having to monitor everything I say and worry our conversations will be stolen . . ." Reid says, lacing his fingers behind his head. "You're the most trustworthy person out there."

I narrow my eyes, his words surprising. I've never thought about my unreadability this way. It's benefited me, that's for sure, but I didn't consider how others might view it. "Prove it then," I say with a smirk, expecting he won't answer. "Tell me a secret."

Reid doesn't hesitate. "I sent Ryder on a job to Blare. She should be safe until we get back."

CHAPTER 7

A cool breeze blows through our makeshift camp, but I feel warmth spreading from deep inside me at Reid's words.

"The job will take her team a while, especially with the travel involved. Ryder is brave but she's so small—"

"And if Bray attacks Madame, Ry will be the first one running toward Craewick," I murmur.

Reid nods. "We both know Ryder will find her way there eventually, but if she's delayed, maybe she'll have a shot at living even if things go wrong with Porter."

My stomach twists at the thought of just how wrong things could go with Porter, and I press my lips into a line. "I wish I knew you better. Then I could tell if you were lying."

He draws closer and holds his hand out.

For a few seconds, I just stare at him, shocked he's willing to let me inside his mind. If our roles were reversed, there's no way I'd do the same. I place my hand in Reid's, his skin tingling as he lets his guard down, and I close my eyes.

At the tip of his mind is a picture of Ryder. She's standing with a few other Shadows in the woods, a dark pack swung across her shoulders. Seeing Ry comforts me, but Reid's emotions are far more powerful. People lie but the feelings weaved within memories never do. I feel his protectiveness—how grateful he is to have found a way to keep her safe.

I can't help but smile as I drink in the memory and open my eyes before slipping my hand out of Reid's. Pride swells up inside me as I think of Ryder, and it's difficult to tell where his emotions end and mine begin. We're both proud of her, strengthened by her fearless, loyal spirit.

For a moment, everything goes away. The throbbing in my head dulls, and the fear of more Minders finding us vanishes. All that matters is somewhere out there, Ryder is traveling far away from the upcoming battle for the Realms.

"Ever since I recruited Ryder, you're all she's talked about," Reid says as he sits across from me once again. "But she never told me your name until last night when she begged me to help your mother. She just always called you her best friend."

I frown. Though Ry's words tug at my heart, Reid's words confuse me. "You mean you haven't read Ryder's mind? You never saw me in her memories?"

"I only read her once to prove she'd be loyal to the Shadows. Like I said, most people deserve to keep their secrets. Everything I know about her and you, I let Ryder tell me herself." He smiles a little. "And you're her hero."

I try not to act too surprised to hear him talk this way, so different than most other Sifters. "Let me see if I have this straight. You're choosing to trust me because Ryder trusts me?" At his brief nod, I add, "I must be a huge disappointment for you then."

He pauses. "You're stronger than you think, as those Minders found out the hard way."

"That wasn't me though. Just a skill I stole."

"That's not the kind of strength I mean. I know how you've protected Ryder and your mother all these years. You've given up everything for them, even your freedom."

I wrap my cloak tighter around me as the wind picks up, blowing leaves around my feet. If he only knew how my mother fell into her coma in the first place, I'm guessing his opinion of me would quickly change. "You don't know anything about me, Reid."

"Oh, but I do. Parts of you . . . or how you used to be, anyway."

"How I used to be?" I say flatly.

Reid grins. "Just a bit more charming than your

current delightful self. I've heard a lot of stories about you, and not just from Ryder."

"I'm sure Bray had a lot of nice things to say."

"Actually, he told me you were a lot like his brother. Hard to train but a quick thinker. The things that irritated him were the reasons you were a good Shadow."

"Sheer defiance?"

He meets my smirk. "Fearlessness. Every time you annoyed Bray, you made up for it in talent."

"Every time we annoyed Bray," I repeat, "we made up for it by doing scout duty in the dead of winter and cleaning out the washhouses. I've gone to bed without supper more times than I can count."

Joss and Penn were always asking Bray for tips and following through on orders, but Cade and I knew the backlash of pushing boundaries wouldn't ruin our lives. Except one day, the fight that was so much a part of Cade got him killed.

"Because the boy fought back, my Minder slit his throat," Madame told me after Greer was captured, *"And the girl, Joss? Well, she got an arrow through her heart. Those stupid children didn't know when to surrender."*

Reid picks up a twig and strips the bark off. "Bray was tough because he believed in you, just like you believe in Ryder."

"Ry's pretty easy to believe in. If she's not helping me sew Minder uniforms, she's off finding another orphan a safe place to sleep or picking berries in the woods to give to the Ungifted beggars," I say. "Did you know she visits my mother every day? She tells her funny stories about the Hollows, acts them out so loudly the nurses kick her out more often than not."

It's the first time I've heard Reid laugh. It's faint, but deep and true. There's a flutter in my stomach, so brief I almost miss it.

"Ry does have one weakness though," I add.

His eyes shift back and forth, as if he's pulling up memories of Ryder. "Blind trust?"

"Blackberry jam. She'll polish off an entire jar in one sitting." I find myself grinning when he laughs again. "Her nana taught her how to make it, and Ry taught some of the orphans so they have something other than their minds to sell on the streets. She wants to be a teacher like my mother when she grows up."

Reid tips his head towards me. "Nah, she wants to be a teacher like *you*. You taught her everything. You gave her a family and kept her safe."

My smile fades as I realize things with Ryder can never go back to the way they were. Life in Craewick was difficult and uncertain, but we'd fallen into a rhythm of looking out for one another. She and my mother gave me a reason to get up every day.

"Maybe I shouldn't have encouraged how much she hates Madame," I say. "I never expected Ry to join the

Shadows. Now she'll be on the run, acting as Bray's puppet."

"But freedom isn't always a lack of strings, right? People can look like they have all the freedom in the world, but they never feel any kind of peace. Ryder's fighting for what she believes in. Isn't that why you pledged to Greer?"

"It was different." I shudder at the thought of Madame staring down Ryder at the auction. "I didn't have Madame's eyes on me back then."

"You also didn't have the chance to knock Madame off her throne. Ryder deserves to play a role in this," he says. "You'll meet up again one day. Family always finds one another."

I touch the pendant on the necklace, tracing the crest of the Woodland Realm with my finger. "You honestly believe that?"

"Why shouldn't I?"

"Because you're a Shadow."

"It's too much of a risk to ever return to your home, even to visit loved ones," Greer told all new recruits. *"If the Minders suspect your family knows your location, they'll torture anyone you care about until they find the answers they're searching for. Your loved ones don't deserve that. Joining the Shadows calls for sacrifice."*

Reid shrugs. "Today I'm a Shadow, but if things go according to plan, I'll find my family again one day."

It's a nice thought, and I wish I could say the same. Not spend the rest of my life working off my debt to Bray. "Where is your—"

He holds his hand up. "How about you answer a question of mine, and I'll answer a question of yours? You're doing all this to save your mother. Where's your father?"

I fiddle with the hem of my tunic. Opening up about Ryder is one thing, but I'm not sure this is a game I want to play. Though I can't deny being curious about Reid's past, even his present. What drove this Sifter to give up his freedom? If I answer his question, I can ask one of my own.

"My father left before I was born," I finally say.

It used to be hard to tell people that, but tonight I'm thankful for how it implies I don't know anything about him. As a child, I hated him for leaving us, but my emotions changed as I got older. They say the opposite of love is hate but it's not. It's apathy. When I joined the Shadows, that's how I felt about my father—a whole pile of nothing.

Everything changed once I learned the truth about him.

"What's your family like?" I ask.

He takes a long drink of water, then kneels by the stream to refill his bottle. "My father died when I was a kid. My mother is Ungifted like yours, and I have a brother and a sister. Both younger."

"Figures. You've got that protective older brother thing about you."

A muscle in his jaw jerks. "Can't protect them from everything."

It doesn't seem like he's speaking to me anymore, not with this sadness in his voice. I'm about to ask what he means when he catches me staring and says, "You should get some sleep."

"I'm not tired," I say with a shrug.

"Okay, then how about making yourself useful?" Reid takes a vial of black liquid out of his pack and quickly whittles a twig to a sharp point. "I can't wipe everyone's mind who sees us in Aravid. If Porter sends Minders after us, I'd rather they start their search for me in the barracks of Kripen." He holds out his wrist. "Ryder says you're an incredible artist. Care to make a proper Sifter out of me?"

As I brush my finger across Reid's wrist, a shiver courses down my spine. The plainness of his skin is a death wish on a Shadow job, a giveaway that he hasn't pledged to the Minders. Though it's easy enough to draw a couple of fake tattoos to disguise Reid as a soldier, Porter will still have our faces in his memory. And I'm not sure any amount of tricks can keep me hidden from someone like him. I bat the thought away, refusing to dwell on anything beyond stealing the map of the Maze.

"So, Commander, where would you like to have never grown up?" I ask Reid.

He grins. "I've heard good things about the coast. Lots of sweet, even-tempered girls."

"Your flattery is going straight to my heart." I bat my eyes like I've seen barmaids in Craewick do, and his smile grows. "The Coastal Realm it is, then."

Though I memorized it long ago, I dip the twig into the ink and close my eyes, recalling the crest of my home. An anchor surrounded by the colorful coral of the Blarien Sea.

The same crest is on my journal, the last gift my mother gave me before I joined the Shadows. She'd tucked scraps of unwanted paper from her classroom under her cloak for months before having enough for pages and even bought a tiny lock to seal it up, the key to which I wore on a piece of string around my neck until I moved to Craewick. I kept the key hidden after that. I was always afraid Madame would notice and steal something else that belonged to me.

Nowadays, I only pull out my journal in the dead of night, after Ry goes to bed. I haven't made many Craewick memories that I feel are worth writing down, so the entries are few and far between.

But every day when I was a child, my mother would write in her own journal and encourage me to write in mine. I filled it from cover to cover with things I'd learned, or people I'd met. How a soft breeze felt on warm cheeks, or a how my mother's hand fit perfectly around mine.

"Write everything down, Julietta. Your memories are a gift, one of the most precious items you own. Each one is completely and utterly unique. Never let yourself forget anything. Always stay my darling little girl."

The journal is in my cottage, locked up and hidden among my mother's dresses. The leather cover is soft and worn now, barely able to bind the scraps of paper, and I always planned to give it to my mother when she wakes. Then she'll know how much I remember.

As Reid's tattoo comes to life, so do the memories of Madame's soldiers. "There was something off about one of those Minders. His mannerisms, the way he spoke, how he said my name . . . it was almost like I was looking straight at Madame," I tell him. When his mouth presses into a line, I quickly add, "It sounds crazy, I know."

"Not crazy. I felt something too. It took me a few seconds to knock them out, like there was some kind of barrier around their minds."

"Unreadability?" I ask, tracing over the thinner lines to darken them.

He shakes his head. "They weren't like you. I heard a bunch of thoughts instead of none . . . almost like I was reading two minds at once. I guess it could be a Gift variation, but the chances that three of Madame's scouts have the same one seem impossible."

"Unlikely, but maybe not impossible," I say slowly, leaning back to study the design on Reid's wrist. "My old Shadow partner had a variation. He had the ability to duplicate memories without losing the original. He could make as many copies as he wanted."

Reid raises his eyebrows. "Sounds like a valuable variation."

I nod. Below the crest of the Coastal Realm, I draw an eye to signify Reid's fake position within the Minders. "Once we stole a skill, we could pass it around to whoever needed it," I say, part of me wanting to talk about Penn forever while the other half just wants to forget the pain of watching him die. "I'm not sure he could duplicate variations, though. Those seem like they're connected to our Gifts, not memory."

"Well, worst case scenario, Madame has figured out how to duplicate variations, or we're dealing with something else entirely. But whatever it is, we'll be ready for them." When I'm done with his tattoos, Reid blows on his wrist to dry the ink. "Looks good."

"They aren't perfect, but they'll pass at a glance," I say.

"Don't sell yourself short. You're quite an artist," he says between breaths. "Thanks for doing this."

"No, thank you," I say. "For everything."

Reid's smile lights his eyes. "You're welcome for everything." He leans against the tree across from me, his gaze out in the woods to keep watch. "Try to rest. Long day ahead of us tomorrow."

The steady sound of the stream, the water dripping

between the rocks, helps soothe me. Closing my eyes, I match my breaths to Reid's deep ones, struggling with these emotions that make me want to laugh and cry all at the same time. What he's doing to me, I don't know. I remember how it felt to trust my Shadow team, to know that they'd always have my back no matter what. That's not how I feel about Reid. But maybe erasing me from the minds of those Minders and his care for Ryder have given me the tiniest flame of hope that we can be allies.

CHAPTER 8

When I fall asleep, I drift back to my tiny room in the Mines, my bed pushed against Joss's. She never talked a lot, probably because Cade and I rarely stopped. But in the drowsiness of night or the wee hours of morning, Joss would open up.

In the midst of our storytelling, we swapped images—just enough to fill one another's minds with any emotions too hard to explain. I bared my very soul with Joss, and through memories, she showed me hers.

Most nights, Cade and Penn would tiptoe into our room, and we'd form a circle on the dusty floor. As we held hands, our fingertips would buzz with our Gifted energy. While Ungifted children played with toys, we played with memories.

We put on shows for one another night after night, spending hours slipping the skills we'd stolen between us. Our veins would light on fire for a few seconds as our bodies adjusted to someone else's years of practice. Then we knew exactly what to do. Talents were only a pile of memories—instruction and experience. Once we remembered how it felt, our muscles were quick to respond. It was all about mimicry, and our Gifts allowed us to do it flawlessly.

One minute Joss would be screeching out notes, and the next she'd sing beautifully. Cade would act out a dramatic monologue, his words executed with just the perfect amount of flare. I'd make Penn waltz with me, our arms and legs graceful and fluid when neither of us owned a drop of natural rhythm.

Life with the Shadows was always thrilling, giving into the rush that our Gifted bodies craved.

"Etta?"

I crack one eye open.

"Sleep well?" Reid asks.

"Never better." I yawn and massage my aching neck, surprised I actually fell asleep. "Must be the frigid temperature and the pleasant company. That comforting threat of Minders, Hunters, Ghosts . . ."

"It must be. I tried waking you earlier, but you didn't even stir. So I checked to make sure you were still breathing and you definitely were . . . drooling too."

I meet his eyes. "I don't drool."

"Bet you think you don't snore either."

"Because I don't!"

He shrugs. "You keep my secrets, and I'll keep yours."

Hiding my smile, I glance up at the trees. They're bursting with leaves, gold and shiny like the coins often discarded for riches of the mind. As the sun spreads its long fingers above us, it's a glorious flood of pink and orange as bright as Blarien coral.

I close my eyes, reminded of something Penn told me long ago.

"They say memories are the same as living it," he says, swinging his arm around me. "But you have to admit, Jules. Real life is so much better."

The woodland birds chirp and tweet, and I smell the clean scent of pine. The stream glitters in the sunlight, the tiny waterfall flowing down a cluster of rocks. It's quiet and peaceful, two things impossible to find in Craewick. There, I longed for the busyness to keep my mind moving. Today I don't mind waking to this world.

Reid kneels beside me. "I want you to take my memories of where the Mines are located." He offers his hand. "If something happens to me, you need to be able to find your way back alone from anywhere in the Realms."

I wave him off. "Nothing's going to happen to you."

He takes my hand anyway. "Look, if Porter is as grand

a manipulator as everyone claims then we can't take any risks. I'm a Sifter, but I'm not arrogant enough to think I don't have threats."

I feel a stab of fear at his words. I'm terrified that Porter will find a way to outsmart me, but it's the first time I've questioned what will happen to Reid if we fail. I tell myself that I can't worry about him too, that he's willingly thrown himself into this mess and can take care of himself. But I have to admit there's some part of me that feels his fate shouldn't be connected to mine.

Closing my eyes, I let his memory sink into me. The Mines are nearer to Craewick than I guessed. Less than half a day's journey to that city in the east and a day to Kripen in the south. Two days from Aravid in the north and Blare in the west.

We keep a quick pace as the sun rises high above us, shedding much needed light as the trail twists and bends. I shift my gaze to the side of his face, to the dirt beneath our boots, to the birds darting just above our heads.

"Do I really snore?" I ask.

Reid smirks but doesn't look at me. "No."

"Thank goodness. 'Cause you do."

He stops walking. "Do not."

"Don't worry." I smile. "Your secret is safe with me."

"What a comfort."

We make it a few more hours before purplish-gray clouds roll in, stealing the day's warmth. I dig through my pack and layer on another shirt. Thunder rolls in the distance, the scent of rain heavy in the air.

"I'd give it an hour before we're soaked," I mutter.

"Generous. I'd give it half that."

Reid's right. My cloak wards off some of the rain, but with each gust of wind, I'm soaked through. We hike up the winding trail, climbing so quickly my legs burn. I scream as thunder claps just above us.

"Always so tense," Reid says with a laugh.

"Nah. I'm on my way to steal a memory from a madman," I say. "What do I possibly have to worry about?"

I expect him to laugh again, but instead, his lips form a grim line.

Turning my back toward him, I climb up the trail, bombarded by questions to which there are no answers. How will Reid ever stay safe from Porter after this job? And how will rummaging through Porter's mind affect me?

When I was younger, I didn't realize how memories stick with you. Change you. Mess with your emotions. Looking back, there's a lot I wish I'd never seen, heard, or felt. That's why I've hardly used my Gift in four years. But once I steal Porter's memory, once I'm exposed to his thoughts and feelings, will I ever be able to separate *him* from *me*?

The memory I once stole of Porter flashes before me. My chest tightens, and I can't breathe as my vision darkens around the edges, trapping me within the memory . . .

I scream as the Minders drag me before Porter, sitting on a throne chiseled from stone. His eyes are as black as night, the gold flecks catching the firelight as the Minders throw me down to bow before him. Pleas for mercy pour from my lips as I wait for sudden darkness to take me.

People say that Porter will erase your every memory with one glance. And he does terrible things down in the Maze. Stuffs his prisoners full of the memories people paid to get rid of, then tortures them mind, body, and soul.

I clutch my chest as my blood turns to fire, coursing through every vein as he breaks into my mind. Crying out, I beg for clemency, for his forgiveness that I slapped a Minder for stealing memories from my baby. But when I lift my head, I know my words will do nothing. I've never seen a smile like his . . . as if he's soaking up every bit of my agony.

I blink, coming back to the present. I don't know who the memory once belonged to, but I accidentally stole it from a Ghost who'd blindsided me back when I was a Shadow. I'm trembling so badly that I can barely put one foot in front of the other. But as the memory fades into the recesses of my mind, I think of my mother in her asylum bed and keep moving forward.

Gradually, the forest of lush, colored trees becomes one of tall evergreens, with tight needles that do little to protect us from the rain. The thick mud on the trail cakes my boots almost instantly, weighing me down.

"At least we'll be able to see footprints if Minders passed this way," Reid says.

I groan in reply, cursing the endless storm. When Reid's jacket spreads across my shoulders, I don't bother telling him to keep himself warm instead. I know so little about Reid, but I'm already confident in the fact that it's pointless to argue with him.

"So, what do you like to do for fun?" he asks.

"Are you trying to distract me?" I glance back at him, water dripping down my face as I roughly wipe it away. "I assure you nothing can put me in a better mood right now."

"Actually, I was hoping you could distract me." He crosses his arms, shirt wet against his chest. His hands are shaking but he smiles. "There has to be more to your life than sewing Minder uniforms, Jules. What's the first thing that comes to mind?"

Calling me Jules throws me a little, but I can't say I hate how it sounds coming from him. "I don't know."

"You do.

I sigh. "Drawing. Sketching portraits, I guess."

"Portraits," he says, amused. "Did you create the skill yourself . . . or steal it?"

"As flattering as that accusation is, no, I didn't steal it. My mother taught me how to sketch," I say as the trail widens enough so he can walk beside me. "She was training to be a teacher in Aravid but moved to Blare after my grandparents died. She wasn't rich enough to buy any artistic talents, so she had to learn all the skills herself before she got a job teaching art to the Collectors. It took her years to master the techniques of drawing and painting, but she loved every minute of it. We'd practice for hours together too. Actually, paper was the first thing I stole from the Minders."

He nudges my arm. "Well, well, Miss Lark, the truth finally comes out. You were a Shadow from the start."

"Toying with the Minders has always been a little too tempting."

"Mmm, I know the feeling. And you never sold your talent? It would've been worth a fortune in Craewick."

I shake my head. "All those memories are some of the best times I spent with my mother. I used to think the Hollows didn't keep skills long enough to develop affection, but my mother always said affection grows long before you master something new. It's in the roughness that love blooms."

"Sounds like a wise woman," he says. "So, what's your favorite thing to sketch?"

"Mostly I draw my mother. Picturing how strong she was reminds me she'll wake up one day."

"And in a world far different than the one she fell asleep in," he says, a bit of hope in his voice. "I have a confession. I saw some of your drawings when I broke into your cottage. You're good, really good."

I give him a tired smile. "Unfortunately, I don't think Bray has much use for charcoal sketches."

"But if things go according to plan, we'll need a replacement for the auction."

Reid says it so seriously that I laugh, and he grins. It's such a funny thought, the grumbling Hollows thrilled at the prospect of a portrait. "Will I get a special booth?" I ask.

"Oh, I'll make sure of it."

Smiling, I take the hand he offers and step over a fallen log on the trail. His skin is warm and tingling against mine, and the fact that his guard is down surprises me. I let go as soon as I'm back on solid ground, not wanting Reid to think that I might try to steal something.

After he crosses over the log, Reid sinks down into a puddle that I avoided. He tries to step out of it but doesn't move. "My foot's caught on a root or—" he says before he trips, splashing mud all around us.

Gasping, I rush toward him and pull on his arm to help him up.

"I'm fine, Etta. Just fine," he says, sounding muffled as he pushes himself onto his feet. He's soaked from head-to-toe, dripping with brown muck. He blinks twice, a look of shock on his face.

I cup my mouth, quivering with laughter. I'm trying so

hard to stop, but once I see he's okay, I lose it completely. Blame it on the lack of sleep, on all the craziness that's happened the past two days, but I can't catch my breath.

"You think this is funny?" Reid says, taking a step toward me before he wipes both his arms off and slings the mud at me.

It gets *everywhere*. In my hair, all over my clothes, and in my mouth. I sputter it out, but when he laughs, it sets me off again. It's a few minutes before we both stop, and I can't remember the last time laughter made me forget. Forget about my mother's coma, forget about Greer. Forget about Cade, Joss, and Penn. Well, maybe forget isn't the right word. Being with Reid is helping me remember all the good parts.

I dig through my pack and hand Reid a rag. "You need it more than I do."

"If you could see yourself, you'd know that isn't true," he says, wiping off his face.

With a smirk, I bend over to shake all the mud out of my hair. "Okay, my turn, right? I told you how I love drawing, now I get to ask a question. Don't expect me to pour out my life story without getting something in return."

Reid's teeth look especially white against all the mud. "My words come back to haunt me. What a burden to have Gifted friends."

"We're not friends." It's true, but it slips out before I

116

think about it. That said, I don't know why I'm worried about hurting his feelings.

"We could be."

I loop my tangled hair into a bun. "Having similar goals doesn't make people friends. After this job, I won't move forward if—"

"If you don't break ties with your past? But I'm not in your past."

"You will be."

"We'll see."

My cheeks burn at his stare. "Bray's right about me, you know. I betray everyone I love. And those are people I love, so where would that leave you, Reid?"

He pauses, then shoves the rag into his pack. "You can't let Bray get to you like this. You left the Shadows four years ago, Etta. Don't you think people can change?"

I skirt past him. "Some things are too wrong to make right."

"You know, running from a fear only intensifies it," Reid calls after me.

"I'm not running from my fear!"

"You're running from me. Same thing."

Hearing him behind me, I spin around. Reid is standing so close I'm terrified he's going to kiss me. Tingles run up and down my spine once I realize I'm not sure I want him to move away. And I can't help but wonder what his lips would feel like pressed against mine.

He doesn't say anything but grins before moving ahead.

And when I realize it's the first time he's let me keep watch, a smile slips across my face.

CHAPTER 9

The rain is barely a drizzle as a dense fog rolls in, turning spidery branches shimmery in the moonlight. It's pretty, this softness that's come over the woods. The mist reminds me of the humid nights spent on the beaches of Blare, and my breath turns to puffs of white as the temperature dips.

I'm also reminded that winter—the numb season, as we Shadows called it—is soon approaching. When you can't feel your fingers or toes, and your mind gets foggy from the bitter cold. The Hollows will pile on even more layers, and swiping memories will be nearly impossible. Even our Gifts, our warm and tingling skin, won't cut through the chill.

Back when I was a Shadow, the numb season always

brought a lot of reprimands from Bray because we'd be tempted to run on the icy streets and make stupid decisions to get home a little sooner. We didn't think clearly, and one of those times, I led a Minder straight to our base.

As soon as I spotted the tree where a scout was waiting to lead me back to the Mines, I ran straight to it. I hadn't bothered to check with the scouts high in the branches, who would've warned me that I was being followed. *You're rash and ignorant,* Bray had yelled at me later. I couldn't argue with him. I'd never even realized a Minder had been trailing me.

The scout saw him right away, shooting an arrow into the Minder's thigh to keep him there until Bray could erase his memories of me. But when Bray arrived, Greer was with him too . . .

"Where are you stationed?" Bray asks the Minder.

No answer.

"Does Madame know where you are?"

I shift my feet. Bray isn't the type of person who usually asks twice, let alone the type you make wait.

Then the boy clutches his head, wrought with pain.

"Bray," Greer says in a voice full of warning. "Enough."

"Madame doesn't know he's here," Bray answers as the Minder sucks in a long breath, his eyes bloodshot from Bray reading his mind. "Doesn't change the fact that we can't let him go. He's a murderer."

Greer glances at me, a quick look up and down as if accessing for injuries, but the soldier hadn't laid a hand on me. "Erase his memories of us and set him free. I won't punish a man for a crime he hasn't committed."

"A crime he hasn't committed yet," Bray shoots back.

Greer takes Bray aside with a rough jerk on his elbow. "Why did you pledge to me, to the Shadows?" When Bray flinches, it's the first time I've even seen him look small. Greer shakes him once. "Answer me. Why?"

"Because I believe in your leadership. I believe in what we're fighting for," Bray says. "I want a better life for my brother. For Cade to grow up in a world where he doesn't have to live in fear."

"Those are the same reasons he joined the Minders." Greer nods toward the soldier. "He has a family too. He has hope and convictions, all of which he's willing to die for. Madame murders Shadows when given the chance, but there will be a difference between her and me, between her Minders and us." He lets Bray go, and Bray stumbles back. "Don't ever forget that."

I blink twice, breaking free of the memory. When I think of Greer, that's the face I see. Not one of anger, not one twisted with revenge like Bray's. I see him showing mercy to someone who never expected it. And I fed him straight to the beast.

Reid and I come across a small cave long after sunset and make camp. It's higher off the ground, tucked into a hill. We're careful to check about, making sure no person or animal had the same idea as us. No signs of a recent fire, no tracks in the soft dirt floor. Just smells faintly of pine. It'll be impossible to keep the chill out, but a roof over our heads is a luxury we won't pass up.

There's a small pond outside, and though the water is freezing, we're desperate to clean the mud off. I work on my hair, my neck, and my face while Reid wades in up to his waist, washing himself and his clothes all at once.

"We should be in Aravid by morning," he calls over. "I've been curious about that city for years. The entire time I've worked for Bray, I've never seen a memory of what lies behind the gate. Do you remember what it's like?"

I shake my head. "I've been in the woods surrounding it, but Greer never let us get too close. Porter wasn't an enemy he wished to make."

Aravid has always been well-protected. A huge, wooden fence encompasses the entire city with an iron gate that hardly ever opens. Tying the end of my braid, I think of the bidder at the auction, of how Madame scoops up Aravid memories before anyone else can. Now that we know she's planning to attack the other Realms, I understand why. I'd want as much information about my prey as I could find too.

"I've seen Porter's fortress from the hills overlooking Aravid before," I add. "It's this massive structure of polished black stone with jagged points of steel on the roof that blind you when it's sunny."

"Well, we'll find out what it's really like tomorrow," Reid says before disappearing under the water.

If only the thought didn't make me lightheaded. Aravid always seemed silent and frozen to me, as if life had asked permission to enter Porter's property and it was denied. With every step closer to his city, I'm terrified he'll find a way to outsmart us once we're standing before his throne.

I'm shaking from head-to-toe when I enter the cave. The extra shirt and pants in my pack are damp with rainwater, but at this point, they feel wonderful compared to what I had been wearing. I wrap my cloak around my shoulders, then spread my thin blanket across myself and prop my pack against the cave wall to rest against it. I'm exhausted and sore all over, my body longing for sleep.

When Reid returns, we pluck bites off a loaf of bread as I redraw his tattoos, the ink having washed off with all this rain and his frigid bath in the pond.

I decide to break the silence. "I still have a question, right? From earlier?" I ask, outlining the crest of the Coastal Realm on the underside of his wrist.

"Ah. So you do care to know more about me."

"I did right up until you said that."

Reid grins. "I'm listening, Miss Lark. Go ahead."

I fill in the crest with tiny strokes of ink. "How long have you worked for Bray?"

"Three years."

"And why did you pledge to him in the first place?

Sifters don't bow before other Sifters unless they're forced to. What does Bray have that you want?"

He looks out at the moon, and with my fingertips on his wrist, I feel his pulse quicken. "Actually, Bray doesn't have what I want. You do, or at least you will." He takes in a quick breath. "My family is with the Tribes—"

I gasp, messing up the swirl on his wrist. "I haven't met anyone from the Tribes in years!"

Reid smiles a little at my reaction.

The Ungifted Tribes are legendary, rarely mentioned in Craewick. They've always been nomadic, living in the forest between the Realms and functioning fully apart from the Gifts. But after Madame rose to power and the division between the Gifted and Ungifted grew enough where the Tribes no longer felt safe, they disappeared completely. I've known a few who grew up among the Ungifted, but I was only close with one—Penn.

"But you're a Sifter," I say. "Your Tribe kicked you out, didn't they?"

"No, I chose to leave. Once the Tribes discover you're Gifted, it's pretty hard to get anyone to trust you. My family would've left along with me, but I couldn't ask them to give up everything they'd ever known. It took me a long time to realize if I clung to them too tightly, I'd suffocate them. But life with the Tribes was great, very different than life in the Realms. Different mindset too. Nobody sees the point of buying memories when you can create your own. Judging by the whole Ungifted life-style you've adopted, you'd probably love it." Reid plucks a piece of grass from the side of the cave and sticks it in his mouth. "We never focused on mastering one skill but knowing a little of everything. How to grow crops or construct homes, things like that. My brother and I were always competing to find out who could shoot the most game, catch the most fish, build the biggest fire . . . You can guess who won."

"Your brother, of course."

He scrunches his nose.

"And you have a sister too?" I say, smoothing out the lines on his wrist to finish the crest.

"She's thirteen. No, fourteen now."

"Quite the lady, I'm sure."

It's the first time I've seen Reid look scared, even more so than with those Minders.

"I hope not. In my mind, she's still a tiny girl with messy braids and a temper my mother worries she won't outgrow," he says with a sigh. "I miss her. I used to visit them until they moved, just to make sure they had enough food. Enough pelts to keep them warm. Believe it or not, I grew up in a place like the Mines."

"The Tribes live underground?" I ask, starting his eye tattoo. Penn kept this a secret, probably to protect his family, but now the details of his memories—the constant flicker of candlelight in his home, the endless expanse of forest around it—make more sense. "That's how they stay hidden?"

"Clever, huh? I'd been tracking my Tribe for months when I found a trapdoor into the Mines, and the scouts brought me to Bray. That's when I pledged to him in exchange for his help with finding my family. If Madame takes over all four Realms, she'll have the resources to hunt the Tribes." He pauses. "Did you ever hear the rumor that her father's murderer could be hiding among the Tribes? Now it's not only practical for Madame to go after all those untouched memories but personal too."

I nod as a shiver runs down my spine. "The Ungifted talk about his death a lot. They feel like Madame uses it to her advantage, though. It's her excuse for why her Minders are overly harsh, why her laws are so strict."

It isn't hard to imagine with four armies at her disposal that Madame will slaughter the Tribes. There's a strength when things draw near to your heart, the all-consuming power that makes even the impossible come true. Tears sting my eyes as I think of my mother, already trapped in this twisted game Madame is playing.

"But how can I help you find the Tribes?" I ask.

"It's not the Tribes I'm looking for anymore. As long as my mother and sister stay hidden with them, they'll be safe until we take Madame down. I can't say the same for my brother." He meets my eyes. "He's in the Maze."

My heart sinks. "So that's why you're here."

Reid puts his hand on my arm as I inch away, and when I flinch, he lets go. "Bray didn't want you worrying about anyone other than Greer, but I have just as much to lose if we don't get that map."

"Oh," is the only thing that slips out.

"All you have to say is *oh*? Ask me another question. Or two," Reid says.

Turning my back toward him, I put the ink back in his pack. Now it makes sense why he fought so hard to make me feel protected, why he volunteered for this job. Sure, this confirms we're really allies, having goals which are fully aligned. But Reid planted the first seeds of trust between us when he gave me that memory of Ryder and I felt how much he cares for her. Ever since then, my words have seemed to pour out without permission, even in the midst of questioning his claims to want me as a partner.

My stomach clenches as another thought creeps in. Is this the only reason Reid wanted to be friends? Because I'm his way into Porter's prison?

I brush my doubts away, irritated I even care. Despite it all, I've enjoyed sharing parts of myself with him that I haven't spoken about in years. But it's unlikely we'll ever work together again after this job, especially if he leaves the Shadows to find his family. No reason to get attached.

"When was your brother captured?" I finally ask.

"A few years after I left the Tribes. I should've known

he'd come after me," he says, running his hand through his short hair. "I searched Craewick, Kripen, and Blare but couldn't find a trace of him until I pledged to Bray. He discovered my brother had been kidnapped, sold to the Minders, and thrown into the Maze."

I face him, widening my eyes. "Your brother was a Shadow?"

"No. He was Ungifted, not that it matters to Madame." Reid picks up a twig, snaps it in two. "The Ungifted mind is still valuable, right?"

I feel disgusted along with him. Memories can only be shifted around in life, only truly destroyed with death. The Gifted and Ungifted are treated alike in the Maze. They're all trapped inside their own minds, forced to hold and relive horrific memories until they finally die— the deepest kind of torture.

Reid adds, "We've been trying to find the Maze for years. I searched every Minder I came across and discovered Madame's plan to take over the Realms, along with the memory that she knows what really happened to Porter's daughter. That Minder I stole it from was still wearing the necklace Bray gave you." He glances at the pendant before lifting his eyes to mine. "Until you showed up, I'd planned to go to Aravid alone, but there was no guarantee Porter wouldn't double cross me. Your unreadability is the only thing that ensures once you steal the map, he can't take it back."

I twist my hands in my lap. "The thing is, the Minders don't usually keep prisoners for very long. I mean, we don't even know if Greer is still alive, and he's a Sifter. And the Ungifted . . . They can't defend themselves at all," I say, then regret how careless I sound when Reid tenses.

"I understand how important it is to find Greer, and I swear I won't leave you until you're both safe," he says. "But I won't leave the Maze without my brother either. He's alive, Etta. I'd know if he were dead."

Nodding, I've heard of the bond shared between siblings. Cade used to say he could feel Bray's presence, a connection deeper than blood—one of energy and memory. "That's good news. Maybe he is still alive." I pause. "Some people deserve to be set free, right?"

Reid gives me a tired smile.

It's strange how quickly life changes. For four years, I thought I knew exactly what I wanted: for my mother to wake. But now I want Greer to be set free, for Reid to be reunited with his brother, and for Madame to be knocked off her throne. Everything has gotten more complicated, but somehow, more hopeful too.

I yawn. "Well . . . 'night." I'm halfway on my feet when Reid grabs my arm and pulls me back down.

"Nice try," he says. "What about my question? A deal is a deal."

Brushing him off, I say, "A lot of people break those."

"A lot of people keep them too. One question, then you can sleep. Promise."

"One more," I growl, although I'm quite enjoying whatever this is. For just a little while, the worries that haven't left in four years have dimmed.

"So many possibilities . . . embarrassing Shadow stories?" he asks before waving his question off. "Nah, too easy."

"Oooh, I'll throw one in for free," I say. "I once told Joss I'd fallen madly in love with Bray's best friend, a boy with the cutest dimples, named Beau. Once Cade found out, he called me Mrs. Beau for weeks until Beau overheard and orchestrated a fake pairing ceremony, inviting every single Shadow to the celebration." I laugh thinking of the pile of presents and heartfelt toasts. "To this day, I'm pretty sure a few of those Shadows never figured out it was only Beau's excuse to throw a party."

Reid smirks. "So, it's safe to say you're in a pretty committed relationship?"

"Our seven-year anniversary is next month." I grin, but then my chest tightens when I think of how Beau ended up.

He went missing right before I left the Shadows, and we'd heard he was imprisoned in Kripen. Imagining Beau, all dimples and laughs, as a captive of the military base, where criminals are released and hunted to train the Minders, was like day and night colliding. And the only reason I knew Greer was outside of Kripen when I gave up his location to Madame is because he, along with Cade and Joss as I later discovered, was on his way to rescue Beau.

When Reid puts his hand on my arm, I'm already inching backwards.

"I hear it too," I whisper over the sound of snapping branches close by.

On my knees, I peek out of the cave and count eight bodies right below, people dressed in frayed rags and worn boots. Their faces are streaked with grime, and their gnarled hair looks as if it's nesting vermin.

Ghosts.

A furious shudder runs through me as something shiny catches my eye. A metal chain clamped around the neck of a girl who's being dragged like a wild animal.

I grit my teeth. I once knew a Shadow who was a captive of the Ghosts. She was tortured for months but thankfully, couldn't recall much because they took her memories to use as ammo. But I can still hear her screams as she woke from nightmares. The little bits of torture she remembered had been brutal enough to make her cry.

"Wipe that look off your face, Etta," Reid whispers harshly.

I glance over. "What look?"

"Like you're about to throw that rock you're holding at one of them. Put your pack on and let's get out of here."

I tighten my grasp around the rock's jagged edges, afraid if I don't, I'll scream. Pushing myself to my feet, I lean over the edge to get a better view of the captive and slip my pack on.

My heart aches at how much she looks like Joss. Her Shadow parents were auctioned when she was a baby, so Joss was raised by Greer too. Some of my memories were inside her when she died, and some of hers are still inside me. A sister in every way but blood.

"We have to get out of here, not start a riot," Reid hisses, holding out my bow, then seems to think better of it and pulls it back. "Don't initiate, okay? You can't save everyone."

We fall on our stomachs as a bloodcurdling war cry sounds right outside the cave.

Out of nowhere, a man wearing a vest of thick black fur barrels toward the captive. He whips a dagger off his belt and slices the arm off the man jerking her chain.

The Ghost drops to the ground, clutching a bloody stump.

Dozens of Hunters emerge from behind the trees, wearing animal skulls on top of their heads, bushy coats, and furry vests. Rushing toward the Ghosts, they're growling, pouncing, howling, and some have whittled their teeth into sharp points. Others are biting throats and swiping chests with talons sewn into wooly gloves.

I close my eyes as a memory of Bray rushes back to

me, when we were stalked by a pack of Hunter wolves on a Shadow job.

"Hunters are the fastest trackers, seeking prey from miles out. That's why the Minders hire them to gather food, but some never return to any of the Realms," he explains over the howling. "By reading the minds of animals, they become a combination of animal instincts and the unpredictability of our nature. Never trust one. You can only play around with memories for so long before those memories start to play around with you."

I peek outside the cave before Reid yanks me back. There's a Ghost climbing up the trail, his bow and arrow drawn. Maybe we could've stayed out of this, kept hidden during this passing storm. But when the Ghost sticks his red-scarfed head into the cave, my hope begins to break.

It shatters completely when he charges at us.

CHAPTER 10

Reid yanks the Ghost forward and whips his bow out of his hands before the boy finds time to fire.

The Ghost lets out a shriek, but one glance from Reid shuts him up.

I don't know what Reid stole, but the boy looks as if he can't remember how to speak before he collapses.

A hand grips my shoulder, and I spin, kicking my adversary in the stomach. The Ghost loses her footing. I reach for her, but she stumbles backwards out of the cave, falling down into the clash of metal below.

"No!" I scream, furious at how quickly my fighting skill has overpowered me.

Reid groans, and my heart races because I know we're thinking the same thing.

They know we're here now.

I clutch my head, panic rising up inside me. If something happens to me, this memory I'm holding for Porter will be lost forever—our only hope to free Greer. Or if I die, will my unreadability disappear? This memory can't fall into the wrong hands, especially not the Ghosts.

As I close my eyes, energy ignites every joint and muscle as I stop fighting the strength of my combat talent. Memories course through my head, shuffling my vision between the present and the past.

I see Ghosts raiding the fray of Craewick and feel the panic of my neighbors as they rush through the streets, knowing the Minders never arrive in time to help them. Screams pierce the air as Ghosts push inside their homes, ripping memories from the minds of the helpless.

When I open my eyes, I'm not scared anymore. I'm ready.

As if he can hear my thoughts, Reid yells, "Don't engage unless you have to!"

We slip out of the cave, and I catch sight of the captive. Her eyes are narrowed, her hair wild and unruly, and her back is arched like a housecat. It strikes me this is no ordinary prisoner. She's a Hunter too, looking as sly as a fox. This attack isn't random . . . it's her rescue.

The girl makes a run for it, but the chain around her neck twists around a tree stump. She yanks it loose, and I think she's going to escape until a Ghost grabs the end of the chain and pulls. She flies backwards and lands on her back. Tears stream down her cheeks as she claws at the lock, trying to free herself of the metal noose.

The Ghost slips a knife from his belt, brings it to her neck. More willing to lose his captive rather than see her set free.

A memory of Joss flashes before me.

"You know, you're my best friend, Jules."

"And you're my sister," I reply.

Years of pent up rage flare up so quickly I nock an arrow, pick a mark on the Ghost's thigh, and let it fly.

Reid yells my name the second it whizzes past him, and what I've done sinks in. We knew we wouldn't slip out of here without a fight, but I've picked an enemy. My fears are confirmed when a Ghost lunges at Reid.

Reid shoves her off and raises his knife before she charges again.

Swinging my bow onto my back, I grab my knife off my belt as a Ghost and a Hunter come between us. I wrap my hands around the Ghost's thick neck, slamming his forehead into my knee. The Hunter backs off after witnessing this handy trick, and I clutch the hilt of my knife to throw it at him.

Wearing the skull of a wolf, he angles his head, silver eyes gleaming.

I brace myself for his attack, ready to feel his sharp teeth plunge into my neck. But it's an even greater shock when he bows slightly before driving his blade into the Ghost behind him.

Whipping around, I call for Reid, having lost him among the fighters, when the captive screams again. She's still on the ground, trying to lift herself up as her elbows collapse under her. Every bit of me wants to help her, but I fly toward Reid when I spot him through the trees.

He's fighting a trio of Ghosts wielding wooden staffs. He blocks and lunges as they attack him, finally twisting a staff out of a girl's hands before slamming it across her back. He's clearly winning, but I'm not the only one who notices.

The man holding the captive's chain pulls a short axe from his belt and locks his sight on Reid. My arrow's still lodged in his leg, but it isn't enough to slow him down.

He leans back to throw his axe, and my knife finds its target through his palm.

Yelling, he drops the axe and the girl's chain, and I sprint toward him.

Coming up from behind, I latch onto his arm and leap into his mind. Hundreds of images flash before me, passing so rapidly I'm dizzy as the Ghost shuffles his thoughts. His memories are moving too quickly for me to steal anything. Though it's a helpful trick to keep me out of his mind, it comes at a price. Shuffling your thoughts this rapidly results in a splitting headache. He's grimacing, clearly in pain. All I have to do is wait until he can't bear it any longer, and I'll be able to snatch whatever I want.

The Ghost punches the side of my face.

Stumbling away, I feel warm blood trickling down my cheek as the gash from the Minder reopens. The Ghost kicks my back, and my knees hit the ground. He whips me around and wraps his hands around my throat, pressing down hard.

My sight blurs as I force my way into the Ghost's mind and see a picture of the captive. The Hunters' attack sits on the very tip of his consciousness, waiting to be stored with other frightening events.

I work as quickly as I can, slicing apart bits and pieces of his memories. I'm careful to take enough to confuse him so he'll let the captive go. Not enough to manipulate my own emotions. If I take too many of his thoughts, they'll make me hate her as much as he does.

He lifts my head and slams it onto the ground.

Deep, sharp pain erupts in the base of my skull. I pull out of his mind and spend my last bits of energy kicking him. One, two, three times before I pull my bloody knife from his palm and slip away.

My skin buzzes as warmth spreads from deep inside my body, the energy of my Gift set free after years of holding back. But a part of me feels ashamed that in the midst of fighting and theft, I finally feel like me again.

With a dazed look, the Ghost drops the captive's chain and joins the rest of the fight.

With a cry of joy that my trick worked, I rush toward the captive, and she recoils as I jam my knife into the lock around her neck. She stops squirming when I scream that I'm trying to help her.

When the chain falls to the ground, the Hunter grins, her teeth whittled into sharp points.

Reid grabs my arm as he passes, pulling me along with him.

Just before we break out of the chaos, I spy a Hunter kick a knife out of a Ghost's hands before gripping her forearm. She convulses, screaming and gnashing her teeth, but the Hunter doesn't stop driving memories into her head. When she opens her eyes, she takes her knife and plunges it into the back of a fellow Ghost.

A shudder runs through me. If a common Hunter can so easily manipulate, turning an enemy into an ally with only a few memories, how are we ever going to stop Madame?

We twist and curve through a sea of evergreens as we move north toward Aravid. I struggle to keep my footing with all the mud left over from the storm, but I'm careful to stay right behind Reid.

He navigates the forest with such ease that I imagine him growing up with the Tribes, running through these woods as a child while his brother and sister chase after him. He doesn't slow his pace until the lights of Aravid flicker in the distance. We're high up in elevation now, overlooking a patch of forest with the fence surrounding the city dead ahead.

Clutching the necklace, I lean over to catch my breath. I shiver as I realize how real this has all become. Somewhere down there is Porter, a player in a game I never wished to be involved in.

"Are you okay?" Reid asks. He doesn't give me time to answer before he puts his finger under my chin, turning my face this way and that. "Your face is swollen. Black and blue too. You promised you weren't going to initiate. What were you thinking by helping that captive?"

"What was I supposed to do? Let her die?" *Let you die?* I almost add, thinking of that Ghost, only seconds away from lodging his axe into Reid's back. "Why are you so angry?"

"I think you know why I'm angry," he snaps before sighing. "I don't want to lose you."

"You won't. We'll get your brother out of the Maze."

He meets my eyes. "You honestly think that's the only reason I'm worried?"

At his words, my mouth dries up. I remind myself this is a job, and we'll be out of one another's lives once this is all over. What confuses me is I don't like the idea and I'm getting the impression Reid doesn't either. Now I'm fighting to keep my breathing steady, and I think he is too because he turns away, looking toward Aravid.

"We should stop here for the night. If Bray is right about all the measures Porter has taken to secure Aravid, arrows will be flying at us the second we set foot on his land. Only Ghosts and Hunters prefer traveling in darkness," he mutters, glancing back at me. "You're shaking, Etta. Just sit down."

Leaning against the trunk of an evergreen, I wrap my cloak around me. I let out a groan when I see the blood from the gash on my cheek has stained the wool.

Reid pulls a tiny jar of white ointment from his pack, puts some onto his finger, and kneels in front of me. "This is going to hurt," he warns but doesn't give me time to react before dabbing it on my cut. I instinctively pull back, but he holds my neck steady. "We can't let it get infected."

He hands me a piece of white gauze to bandage my cheek, and as I lift it to my face, my heart leaps into my throat. There are only three bracelets on my wrist.

I sit up, frantically searching the ground all around me. Somewhere between battling Ghosts and Hunters, and running through these woods, Penn's slipped off.

Tears sting my eyes as I picture hundreds of places it could be. On the trail? In the pond by the cave? It's the only thing I own that belonged to Penn, a piece of him I swore never to let go. The thought that it's gone hurts in a place so deep that I cry out. It's as if I'm saying goodbye all over again.

"Whoa, Etta, what's wrong?" Reid asks.

"I lost my bracelet!" I say, holding my wrist up to show him the others, but he's already saying, "The leather one? It was by our packs in the cave."

Reid pulls it from his pocket and holds it up.

I hug him so quickly I almost knock him over.

He lets out a soft laugh, sitting down to steady himself before placing the bracelet in my palm and closing my hand around it. "That must've belonged to someone pretty special."

"It was my partner's," I whisper. He's close enough that I see the tiny gold flecks in his eyes, but neither one of us moves. "Cade and Joss were killed near Kripen, but he died in Blare. I owe my life to him." My throat tightens. "He was the bravest person I've ever known. Nothing scared him, not even when he was about to get jumped by a gang of drunken Minders in Kripen. That's where we met."

"Kripen has always been a snake pit, but I guess that's what happens when you have a Realm ruled by a fiend like Declan," Reid says.

I nod. The capital city of each Realm appears to have taken on the personality of their ruler. Sorien of Blare always seemed kind to me, a trait that trickled down to his people, while everything in Craewick is cold and distant. And who knows what to expect in Aravid . . .

"How'd you and your partner get away from those Minders?" Reid asks.

As I put Penn's bracelet on, my memories pull me back to Kripen. From the outside, it resembles any dilapidated city with its paint-chipped buildings and low tin roofs. The porches are missing spindles, mimicking many of the Minders' knocked-out teeth, and the air reeks of human filth poured out onto the dirt roads and the sickening sweetness of ale drifting from a tavern.

The streets are crowded with vendors offering stale bread and less-than-fresh meat, but there's always a gleam in their eyes. A little clue that there's far more on the menu for anyone who wants to barter. Underneath its muck and grime, Kripen is a goldmine for the lawless . . .

I slip down the alley, watching the boy huddled in the corner, his back pressed against the brick wall. He pulls his knees up to his chest, shivering as the last of the sun disappears. His coat is ragged, barely covering his skin, but even from here I can see he's unmarked. No tattoo to indicate whether he's Gifted or not, though I could've sworn I saw him giving a memory to an Ungifted beggar earlier.

The boy had passed by her, his touch lingering on her arm just long enough that I thought he'd stolen something himself. Her eyes had been cloudy, a signal she'd already been a victim of theft or she'd sold too many memories. But when her face brightened, I knew it was just the opposite. He'd given the beggar a memory to strengthen her.

I tiptoe toward him, careful not to get close enough that he could touch me until I know if he's a threat or not. "You shouldn't be here," I call out.

He glances over. "I didn't think I was bothering anyone. You're the first person I've seen in hours."

"Exactly. Being alone in this part of town is like screaming to any thief 'Come and get me,'" I shoot back.

The boy tilts his head to the side. He doesn't look nervous or frightened, only curious. "So you're that thief then?"

"Not today," I reply.

Voices come from the other end of the alley before a group of Minders appears.

The boy pushes himself onto his feet, standing between us. He has no reason to protect me, not with Bray close behind, but the fact that he tries tells me more than his words ever could.

I blink, leaving the memory to meet Reid's stare. "Bray knocked those Minders out before they attacked us, and that boy became my partner, along with Cade and Joss. He was a better Shadow than I've ever been. I don't know why I'm here and he's not—" My voice cracks as I rub his bracelet between my fingers.

After they died, Cade, Joss, and Penn's deaths tainted every memory we had together. A question grew louder and louder in my head each time I thought about them.

Did you ever think this was how things would end?

The way I see it now, the good and bad memories are like a rope, completely intertwined. Pull one strand and the entire thing unravels.

"I know what it's like to lose someone you love. The ache of missing them never really goes away," says Reid.

I look up at him. "So what do we do?"

He smiles slightly. "I guess we learn to love again."

We fall into silence as we lean against two trunks beside one another, staring out over the lights of Aravid. The ground is soft with pine needles, the air sharp with their scent as a cool wind blows through the trees.

"This is it, isn't it?" I whisper, pulling my cloak tighter around me. "Tomorrow we go before Porter."

"I won't let anything happen to you, Etta."

I close my eyes. "Aren't you scared? We have no idea what to expect."

It's a few seconds before he says, "I am scared. But when I think about what happens if we don't do this, I'm terrified. We'll get through this. We have to," he says quietly, then pauses. "How did you discover you were different?"

I glance over at him. "You mean my variation?"

He nods.

"One minute I could be read, the next I couldn't," I say quickly.

"Nothing unusual happened before then?"

A knot forms in my stomach. What do I tell him? My best friend died in my arms after I accidentally put my mother in a coma? "Why do you want to know?" I ask.

"I've always wondered if there could be variations

among the Shadows that we don't know about because they haven't been discovered. If we found a way to pinpoint a variation, maybe we'd stand a better chance of fighting against the Minders. Your mother is Ungifted, and you said you don't know anything about your father. Maybe the variations are passed down in some way?" he prods.

My face warms. I know *where* my variation came from, but I'm not sure how to tell him. "I don't want to talk about this."

"Didn't mean to upset you," he says slowly.

I throw my hands up. "I'm not upset!"

"Then just listen—"

"I am listening."

He rubs the back of his neck. "Why are you getting angry?"

"Because I already know where my variation came from!" I take a deep breath. "Greer is my father."

CHAPTER 11

The look on Reid's face is hard to bear.

"I know what you're thinking," I whisper. "I bought my mother's life with my father's blood."

Before I think better of it, the story of when I first met Greer tumbles out of my mouth.

Just after I turned ten, I noticed my mother's panic when I told her about my nightmares. Her hand tensed on my shoulder as we strolled down the wharf, and her words became constant reminders not to tell anyone how skin tingled beneath my fingertips.

Then one day, my mother began packing up all my clothes and told me a man named Greer had visited her.

"I've known him since before I knew you, Julietta. But each time he visits, he takes the memories of us to keep me safe and returns them when he comes back. Though he's not a friend of the Minders, he can teach you how to use your Gift, my sweet. You'll grow to love him." She kissed my forehead. "I'm certain of it."

"Your leaving will be hazy to your mother," Greer told me when he came a few days later. "But I've left her with enough memories of you that she'll trust you're safe."

At first I was missing my mother so much that I didn't let myself get attached to Greer, but I couldn't help being drawn to him. His hand was sturdy and firm around mine, and though he hardly smiled, the lines of his face were kind. He told me stories and listened when I told my own as we hiked to the Mines. Once I saw the memory market, I was excited about learning to use my Gift.

"A memory contains hundreds of sights, sounds, and feelings which form a picture." Greer held up a seascape of Blare I'd painted for him. "You can give away the entire memory at once." His hand covered half of it. "Or only parts of it. Most think of a memory as a single unit, but it can be broken into smaller bits. Each one is just as power-ful. The energy in your mind knows what to do, but you must tell it how to function."

Like the scissors in my mother's classroom, I learned to slice apart my memories, seeing the images as clearly in my head as I did with my own eyes. My Gifted mind was willing to give away pieces and let me keep the rest. It's how I could show Penn a memory of the beach without forgetting what the sea smelled like or how a gust of humid wind felt on my face.

Then Greer explained how to erase memories from others. "Don't focus on concepts but details. Your mind will get overloaded if you take too many memories at once. It's why the Gifted have headaches and fevers. If I wanted you to forget your mother, I would not try to erase the concept of mothers. You might meet someone else's mother and wonder why you didn't have one. I would erase your own mother's face. How her hand feels on your cheek, the way she tucks you into bed. If I took enough memories, you would remember you once had a mother, but you wouldn't be able to pick her out in a crowd."

The thought terrified me. "Will someone do that?" I asked.

"Not under my watch."

The next week, Greer took me to the auction. It was my first time visiting Craewick, and the only citizens I'd ever met from this city were those visiting Blare to learn artistic skills. They were curious and teachable, often adopting the loose, billowy fashions of Blare and spending their weekends at the beach or learning to fish. But in Craewick, everyone wore long pants and thick jackets with collars pulled up to their ears. They hardly spoke to one another but kept their eyes on the auction block.

Greer explained they were the wealthiest of the

Gifted, their minds filled to the brim in a place where exciting memories were only a touch away.

"Why do you say most of the Gifted are hollow?" I asked Greer.

"Because there's nothing left inside of them."

I frowned. How could he say these people were empty when they were stuffed full of rare talents and thrilling memories? "But there's so much inside of them!"

He touched his heart. "No, nothing is left of them, of who they once were . . . they've lost themselves to become someone else."

"But won't the Hollows remember they bought these memories tonight?" I asked.

"To fully forget, they erase where the memory comes from."

"The transfer?"

Greer nodded. "Memories are like dreams. Once a person falls asleep, that world becomes their life. The Hollows pay to have the auction erased. And if one doesn't remember how the memory was planted inside his head, he'll believe he created it. But memories can only be passed around for so long before a society craves originality and uniqueness. The Hollows have forgotten how valuable our differences are to one another." He patted my jacket pocket, where I kept the journal my mother gave me. "Write, Jules. Write about your day, your every thought and feeling, and all the memories you're carrying. Then you'll always remember who you are."

It wasn't until the auction began that I understood what Greer meant. I'd never seen a Gift be used to end a life, didn't know something I believed was good could be evil too.

The bids rose higher and higher as Madame brought out more prisoners.

With each memory passed between the Hollows, their eyes became glossy and strangely disconnected. Their faces turned ashen. By the end of the night, they seemed to look through me instead of at me.

"Auctions are a sport for the Hollows," Greer said. "If you pledge to the Minders, you'll be under their protection, but the price is your past, present, and future. Madame and the other rulers end the lives of traitors faster than they save the loyal."

A shudder ran down my spine as I slipped my hand into his, and Greer held it tight.

As Madame transferred the memories, I asked Greer how a Sifter's Gift worked.

"When I implant a memory into someone, they feel nothing," he answered. "It simply dissolves into the core of their being. That's why being a Sifter comes with a large responsibility. We can change a person's thoughts in an instant."

"Is this why Sifters rule the Realms? Because people are too afraid not to pledge to them?" I asked.

"Perhaps, but a Gift should always be used to care for and protect those less fortunate than ourselves. Do you know why we're called the Gifted, Julietta? Long ago, memories weren't used like coins. Memories were gifts, to show a glorious sunset to one who'd lost their sight or share music with one who could no longer hear. Somewhere along the way, we became callous and hollow." Greer stared at Madame on the auction stage. "She fails to realize the highest calling we've been given is to serve."

Now I understood the Minders would take more than they would ever give back. My mother had sent me away to offer a future beyond my inevitable conscription into the army or a job working for the treasury. She'd given up our life together to ensure I truly *lived*. Not through memories or purchasing talents, bypassing the joy when you go from failing to succeeding, but so that I would always remember who I am.

And after I swore my life to the leader of the Shadows, Greer told me who he truly was—my father.

A wind blows through the clearing, drawing me out of the past and back to the present. I'm so thankful my mother is alive, but I know I should've fought harder to protect Greer as he'd always done for me.

Tears sting my eyes as I remember Madame, disgust written all over her face, staring down at my comatose mother as we struck our deal. The second I told her Greer's location, a cruel smile had flickered across her face.

You were so easily broken, Julietta, just like your mother.

When I look at Reid, I brace myself for him to tell me what a monster I am.

But all he says is, "Does Madame know he's your father?"

I shake my head. "I don't think so. Besides my mother, the only other person who knows is Bray."

"Madame never read your mother's mind in the asylum?" he asks.

"She could try, but my mother's thoughts are so tangled that she might not even remember who Greer is anymore. If Madame had found out Greer is my father, I think she would've taunted me with that. Instead, she's just always called me a traitor for betraying the leader I vowed to serve."

His arm brushes up against mine. "I don't know what I would've done if Madame pulled something like that on me. You were forced to make an impossible choice," he says quietly. "I know it was difficult to tell me that, but I'm glad you did."

Meeting Reid's eyes, I'm surprised his look isn't cold and distant. If anything, his expression seems softer, and I smile a little, relieved this secret is finally out in the open. "I'm surprised Bray didn't tell you."

He shrugs. "I take orders from him. We're not partners. He keeps to himself a lot."

I pull at a few loose threads on my cloak. Bray's never

been one for small talk, but still, it strikes me as odd. If he kept something this big from Reid, what else could he be hiding?

Reid glances over. "Bray sent Shadows to keep an eye on your mother as soon as he saw the auction notice, even before you made your deal. I didn't understand why until now."

I sit up straighter. "He did?"

"I won't lie to you, Etta. She's not safe yet. Bray can't risk Madame's wrath by breaking your mother out of the asylum until we have Greer, but Bray is watching over her."

The back of my throat stings, though Reid's words comfort me more than he knows. I'm certain Bray will do whatever he can to protect my mother for Greer's sake, but it also feels like a slap in the face. He's a better Shadow than I've ever been. My betrayal is why we're in this mess in the first place while Bray's unwavering loyalty to Greer is what might save us.

Reid inches closer. "Everything will work out in Aravid. Whatever happens with Porter, I'll protect you. I don't rule a Realm, but my Gift is powerful too. We'll get Greer back."

I rub a few pine needles between my fingers. "It's not only failure I'm worried about. What happens if we succeed? Porter is a madman. He's violent and heartless, and I'm scared . . . no, I'm terrified of rummaging inside his mind." I let out a grim laugh. "But maybe I shouldn't care. Porter and I aren't that different anyway."

"What does that mean?" he asks flatly.

Guilt pinches my stomach. "You know the Minder who attacked me? I was going to steal the memories of his newborn son as leverage. So what's the real difference between a manipulator like Porter and me, Reid? He takes people's lives and I take bits of their lives, but we're both thieves." I pause. "You were right about me, you know. The only thing I'm good at is stealing what people love the most. I'm the perfect thief."

Reid sighs, his shoulder still pressed against mine. "Etta—"

"Goodnight, Reid," I say and turn away to grab my blanket from my pack. My back toward him, I curl up with my blanket and bring my knees to my chest, shivering on the cold dirt.

After a few minutes, Reid moves his pack to his other side, leaving the space between us open. "If you're cold, it's okay to come over here."

I bristle. People in Craewick don't usually get so close. Not when we pass memories so easily and lose precious items if we're not careful. Even though I can't be read, it's a habit I've kept up. But as the wind blows, cutting through my cloak, I sit up and tuck myself against him, my head on his shoulder.

Reid puts his arm around me, drawing me a little

closer. Even through his clothes, the heat from the energy in his skin makes all the difference.

As I relax against him, I feel his heart beating steadily. I wish his calm and confidence would rub off on me. With Reid as my ally, I really want to believe we'll get through this. I let out a long breath. How would I've survived out here if Bray had let me do this job alone? Seems foolish I even demanded it now.

Closing my eyes, I refuse to think about tomorrow, knowing if I do that I'll work myself into a panic. Greer taught me long ago how to compartmentalize memories. It's a trick so we're not constantly plagued by others' thoughts, and it's how I've kept the memories of Cade, Joss, and Penn buried for four years. But the memories of my mother, I always kept near. So just before I fall asleep, I return to Blare.

I scrunch cool wet sand between my toes as the balmy air kisses my face.

The waves are soft and low as the seabirds fly just above our heads, their calls mixing with the sound of my mother's voice.

Softly singing, she swipes her brush across her canvas, painting a scene as beautiful as the one spread out before us . . .

And just for a little while, I'm home.

Reid stirs sometime later, and I wake with a dull burn in

my belly, always finding the happiest memories leave the sharpest pain as they fade away. But reliving the years I spent with my mother has done something else to me too. It fills me with strength, the reminder that all is not lost. She still has a life to live.

We have three days to free Greer, four until the auction, and not a moment to lose. And today, I can't let even a sliver of doubt inside me.

I push myself to my feet, shivering as I leave the warmth of being close to Reid.

"Etta, about what you said last night," he says, sitting up against the tree.

As I stuff the blanket back into my pack, I meet his eyes.

"I don't know what you'll end up doing with your life, but now that I know you . . . a little," he smiles slightly as if expecting me to remind him that we're not friends, "I'm positive you can be so much more than a memory thief."

A heavy weariness creeps over me. "I wish I could believe that myself," I say quietly.

"Well, until you do I'll believe it for you. How you see yourself isn't how I see you," he says. "And if something goes wrong with Porter, I wanted you to know that."

"Nothing's going wrong today, Reid." My throat tightens as I swing my pack onto my back. Part of me wants to wrap my arms around him, to tell him that his words mean so much more than I care to admit. But I plant my feet, reminding myself our job together is nearly over. I glance toward Aravid. "Let's get this over with."

With the morning sun, our view of Aravid is even more daunting. Down the hill is another patch of forest, behind which lie the gates of Aravid. They're huge barriers made of swirling iron, and surrounding the city is the tallest wooden fence I've ever seen. There are dozens of Minders patrolling the perimeter and standing watch high in the guard towers.

It's impossible to tell if all this security is meant to protect Aravid citizens or keep them trapped inside. We don't have gates and fences in Craewick. The fear of the criminals lurking in the forest surrounding us is enough to make anyone think twice about traveling without an escort.

"Are you ready?" says Reid, looking far in the distance at Porter's compound, its tall black peaks rising up like swords piercing the sky.

I bite my lip. Am I? I want to say yes, but my trembling hands and racing heart tell another story. Each time I close my eyes, I see flashes of the memory I'll soon give Porter. To share his child is still alive, that Madame has been keeping this a secret from him, is a memory stronger than any weapon. But will it be enough to distract him while I steal his map of the Maze? I can't know the answer until I'm deep within his mind, rifling through his memories. It's still anyone's guess how his thoughts will affect me.

But at the chance to free Greer and my mother, to protect Ryder and save Reid's brother, it's a risk I'm willing to take.

Reid takes my hand, and I feel mine shaking within his as he squeezes it lightly. "We can do this."

I squeeze his hand back.

As we walk out of the forest, no longer hidden behind the tree line, the Minders stationed at the gate narrow their sights on us.

Straightening my shoulders, I clutch the necklace under my cloak and pull it out where they can see it. *Say you know Porter has a daughter. You know who faked her death. And you know she's still alive.* I spy a Minder who's a commander, a thick row of metals pinned onto her uniform, and meet her eyes.

A gust of wind pushes my hood away from my face.

The commander's mouth drops open as she rushes toward me. "Emilia? It can't be!"

I jerk to a halt as a group of Minders follows after her, their hands on the hilts of their knives.

Reid draws closer, standing slightly in front of me.

The commander strides toward us, tears flooding her gold-flecked eyes as she looks at the cut on my cheek. "Oh, Emilia, you've escaped! How?"

Reid's hand tenses on my arm as my blood rushes to my ears. I've never heard of anyone named Emilia.

"Or perhaps you didn't escape." The commander's face

hardens as she looks at Reid. Her stance is rigid, her hand inching toward the knife on her belt. "Who are you, Sifter?"

The Minders behind her step toward us as I dart in front of Reid.

"A friend. I wouldn't have gotten here without him," I say.

The commander raises her eyebrows. "He helped you escape?"

The throbbing in my head worsens at hearing that word again. Hundreds of questions flood my mind, but one sticks out above all the rest. Sometimes I forget I wasn't always unreadable. Is there another past I've forgotten?

A past where Emilia existed . . . and Etta did not?

I clutch a handful of Reid's jacket as my knees give out.

He wraps his arm around my waist to keep me up.

"Take her from the boy," the commander whispers to those flanking her.

"I'm not going anywhere without him!" I scream.

"Don't be frightened, Emilia," she says, her guards still moving toward us before she tells them to stand down. "You don't remember me? I'm Commander Averett."

Memories course through my mind as I search for her name but come up blank. I glance between the Minders, trapping us on all sides. Panic swells up inside me as Reid tightens his grip around my waist. I can't catch a breath as my mind spins, but I order myself to get our plan back on course.

"I wish to see Porter," I say in the steadiest voice I can manage. I don't know anything about this Commander Averett, but if being mistaken for Emilia is enough to get us inside Aravid, does it matter?

She hesitates a moment, staring at me as if she's trying to read my mind. A look of confusion crosses her face before she motions to the guard tower.

As the gate opens, I lose the feeling in my legs completely, my feet dragging behind me as we move toward the gate. Reid is shaking too. The steady, calm temperament I've come to associate with him has vanished. I squeeze my eyes shut, dreading what these Minders will do to us once they realize I'm not the girl they've apparently been searching for.

But what terrifies me more is that perhaps I really am Emilia.

Behind the gate, the Aravid I imagined is nothing like this. I blink twice. At the end of a polished marble pathway lined by all sorts of greenery, thick hedges, and all kinds of fruit trees, there are shops in all shapes and sizes. Most have rounded turrets, painted shutters, and flower boxes below the windows. There aren't any raggedy orphans huddled on street corners, or Hollows wearing outfits protecting every inch of skin. According to the rumors, there should be whipping posts and tight-faced Minders patrolling these cobblestone streets.

I shake my head, feeling as if I'm trapped in a memory. I'm blinking rapidly but nothing changes. This can't be right.

The commander whispers in my ear, "Don't lie if this boy has hurt you. Now's the time to speak up."

"I wouldn't be here without him. He's my friend," I say through my teeth.

Her face tightens. "I'm sorry, Emilia. I wish I could believe that."

A Minder jerks Reid away from me, and another soldier rushes toward them.

Using his Gift, Reid knocks him out as soon as he meets his eyes, but he's struggling to get free of the one he can't see.

"Take him down!" the commander yells toward the guard station.

I send my hand flying toward her throat, but she blocks it and wrenches my arm behind me. I feel our entire plan slipping away—everything we've worked for gone in an instant. Reid's focus wavers when I scream to warn him of the Minders behind him, but I'm too late.

The Minders slip a black hood over his head before cracking an elbow on his temple.

"Let him go," I cry, struggling against her as they drag Reid's limp body toward the guard tower.

She loosens her grip as they disappear.

I push her away, stumbling in the direction they took him. Three Minders block my path, and I whip around to face the commander. "He's done nothing wrong," I shout.

"It may seem to you like he's your friend, but he's a Sifter. A manipulator! He won't be hurt, only questioned." She gestures to my face. "There's a cut on your cheek, all the bruising around your neck . . . he's hurt you—"

"He didn't do this! Minders did," I spit out.

"That's what I'm saying. That Sifter has the eye tattoo. He's a Minder who works for Madame! She sent us word that you were alive, and she was going to kill you if we didn't comply. You were imprisoned by her. You've been missing for years." She motions around us. "Do you remember anything? Anything at all?"

"I've never been here before," I say quietly, furiously.

The commander narrows in on my necklace before she looks behind me and nods. "I'm sorry, Emilia, but you've given me no choice."

Someone pinches the back of my neck and just before blackness envelopes me, I hear a voice full of sadness say, "Poor girl. Madame sure has a twisted sense of humor."

CHAPTER 12

I'm in the Maze.

It's dark, damp, and the air is too thick to breathe. I pass rows of prisoners locked behind stone walls. None of them are Greer. Most of them are bloody and bruised, but the fight hasn't left them.

A man reaches out to me, threats spewing from his mouth as he hits his shackles against the bars.

And I know if I called for help, no one would come to rescue me. They couldn't even hear me with all the prisoners calling for my death.

No, not calling. They're demanding it.

Cade and Joss are at the end of the row. Hands bound, faces ashen. Cade's throat is bleeding, and Joss has an arrow through her heart.

I look down at Penn's head in my lap, at the crimson blood blooming on his white shirt.

He opens his eyes for the last time. "I love you," he whispers. "Never forget me . . . then I'll always be with you."

All three of them vanish. I cry out their names, but no one comes back.

My palm burns as if it's been set on fire. I fling my hand down, but the envelope doesn't move. Instead, *Miss Julietta Lark* slowly burns itself across the front. Each letter is red and shimmering, tiny flames on my mother's Notice of Auction.

I look up. I'm standing in front of the auction block.

Tied to a metal chair, my mother is the only person on the stage besides Madame.

Madame circles her, her fingers trailing across my mother's shoulders.

My mother opens her eyes and screams.

I wake with a jerk. A soft glow fills my eyelids. The floor creaks as a shadow falls over me. I fight against wanting to thrash and scream, forcing myself to remain still.

"Oh, poor dear," a calm voice murmurs. "Commander Averett said she was quite distraught. It's no wonder, with her injuries. She's been through an ordeal to be sure."

No one answers, so I gather he's only speaking to himself. I'm not sure how much longer I can keep up the sleeping act. I clench the soft bedding in my hands, fairly certain a cell in the Maze wouldn't have silk sheets, and order myself to find a way out of this mess.

We only needed one thing before we were trapped inside Aravid's high walls—to steal the map of the Maze. But now what will happen to Reid if I don't find a way to secure his release, as well? I imagine all the ways the Minders could cook up to torture a Sifter and think I might be sick.

There's a rustle of paper before the man mutters, "Maybe it says something in here . . . or perhaps Madame . . ." He sighs. "Oh, dear. Oh, dear indeed. Gwendolyn Lark, it says right here."

My heart pounds so loudly that I'm afraid he can hear it. He's gone through my pack, found the notice. I gasp then curse myself when I hear the man whisper, excitement riddled through his voice, "Oh, she's stirring. I'll fetch Porter. Fetch him right away."

Porter! The stolen memory I have of him flashes behind my eyelids, filling me with terror as the woman's fear mixes with my own. It's overwhelming. I'm about to jump out of this bed just before the kind voice says, "I'm not sure if you can hear me, my dear, but I must say that we feel as if we've failed you. But now that you're here, we shall protect you from now on." His tears drip onto my face as he kisses my forehead. "I promise you that."

The door closes with a soft thud.

Opening my eyes, I lean up on my elbows and gasp. This is no Maze, or at least, not the one I've heard about. Gold sconces cast a warm glow upon the prettiest bedroom I've ever seen, with its floor-to-ceiling windows and thick lavender curtains puddling on the plush rugs. I've been sleeping in a bed with a canopy of swirling silver branches and piles of blankets in rich colors and fabrics.

If I weren't a prisoner, I'd feel quite honored to be here.

Whipping the quilts off, I leap out of bed. My boots and cloak are gone, and the necklace is missing too. I lunge toward the mahogany wardrobe straight ahead.

What stops me cold is the portrait above the fireplace. It's shiny oil on canvas, done with as much skill as I've ever seen from anyone with a painting talent. It's stunning, full of color, dimension, and the most intricate details. I draw closer and blink a few times, certain my eyes are playing tricks.

Because the girl in the painting is me.

My skin feels as if I'm burning from the inside out. I'm drenched in sweat, my clothes stuck to my quivering body as the icy marble sways beneath my bare feet. My heart races as I search my mind for any kind of familiarity, but if my memories are missing, no trace will remain. Still, there are usually scars. Black spots forming a *before* and an *after*.

I pound my fist on my forehead, unable to recall even the slightest seams. I remember every day of my life as a

Shadow and living in Craewick. It all connects perfectly.
So where does a life in Aravid fit in? I clutch my chest,
unable to breathe. Perhaps I never lived here at all and
Porter is an even grander manipulator than I thought
possible.

Darting around the room, I search for my pack to
get my knives. My knees buckle when I see my mother's cloak draped across one of the armchairs in front of
the blazing fireplace. It's been washed and pressed, no
longer stained by the blood from the gash on my cheek. I
pinch the bridge of my nose as a wave of nausea hits me
hard. Who around here would take the time to clean my
mother's cloak?

The small wooden box beside it catches my eye. It
trembles in my hands as I pick it up. It's velvet lined like
a jewelry chest, but inside is a small leather book just like
the journal my mother gave me. But this one is burned a
bit around the edges, the tips of the pages black with soot.

The door creaks open, and I whip around, dropping
the box onto the floor.

I can't move as I meet Porter's stare. He's years older
than in the memory I have of him. There are wrinkles
on his brow, the ringlets on his head now gray, but his
eyes haven't changed. The gold flecks are so bright that
I can see them even from across the room. My stomach
quivers as he walks toward me. I lean against the chair as
my vision darkens around him.

Wearing a dark jacket cut in the same military style as the commander's, Porter is nothing like the elderly in Craewick. His hands don't shake, his gaze isn't aloof. Quite the opposite of feeble, his age serves only to make him intimidating. As if he's seen it all and nothing can surprise him.

Well, perhaps nothing except me. There's a single crack in the tough exterior, a redness around his eyes that hints at his emotions while his face is careful not to.

"It *is* you," he says.

I expect disbelief to riddle his tone, but mostly I hear certainty. I steal a glance at the portrait.

He follows my gaze. "Do you know who that is?"

Biting back a scream, I rub my eyes and order myself not to fall for these mind games, but seeds of doubt about my past have already been planted. My head feels as if it'll split in two as memories of my childhood pulse behind my eyelids.

Is Porter a liar or are my memories a lie?

I feel his hand on my shoulder and jerk away, looking for anything I can use to defend myself. A pair of candlesticks? The quill pen on the desk? I snatch it up and jab it at him. "Stay away from me," I hiss.

His face hardens as he steps toward me once again. "You're quite pale, child. You're going to hurt yourself—"

My laugh sounds hysterical even to my own ears. "You're worried about *me* getting hurt? That's rich coming from someone like you!"

I lunge toward my pack and rifle through it for my knives. I clench my hands into fists when I realize the man who was in here before must've taken them. Now all I've got to defend myself are a few extra shirts and my mother's auction notice, all of which I shove back in before throwing my pack on the floor.

"You're safe now," Porter says. "There's no reason to be frightened. Please just tell me what you remember."

The memory I'm supposed to give him flashes through my mind, my lone bartering chip to secure my release. But I'm too afraid to give it up before I know Reid is safe . . . or even still alive. I squeeze my eyes shut, imagining Porter beside Madame when he agreed to imprison Greer in the Maze. He must know endless ways to torture a Sifter.

I whip around to face him. "Where's Reid? You better not have hurt him."

Porter puts one hand up. "He won't be hurt, only questioned. He's said very little, but perhaps you can shed light on this situation." In my silence he adds, "If you'll only calm down, I'll explain everything."

"I've been warned about you. You *manipulate* people! You're a liar." I jab the pen toward the portrait hanging over the fireplace. "That can't be me!"

"You're right," he says simply. "Sometimes people hope for something so badly that it comes true, if only in their own mind. And that isn't you, Julietta."

"How do you know my name?" My head spins as the floor rolls like the waves of the Blarien Sea. The pen drops out of my hand, clattering onto the marble, and I can't feel my legs.

But before I fall, Porter's beside me, his arms surprisingly strong.

I struggle against him, but I'm too weak to push him away. Tears stream down my cheeks as he helps me sit in the chair beside the fireplace, and I stare up at the portrait.

"Shall I tell you who she is?" Porter asks quietly.

All I can do is nod.

He clears his throat and the faintest of smiles appears on his lips. "It's your mother."

CHAPTER
13

I once knew a girl named Fynn who pledged to Greer alongside her little sister. When we first met, she was bruised all over with deep, angry purple scars on her wrists and ankles. One night, I overheard Bray and Greer discussing who'd hurt her.

Fynn had been kidnapped and sold to a family of Hollows whose daughter had been deathly ill. Just before their daughter died, they planted all her memories inside Fynn. Then they dyed her hair and painted her face, and Fynn lived as another person for years before her sister found her and showed her the truth through their childhood memories. When Fynn tried to escape, the Hollows put her in chains until she found a way to break them.

Back then, I couldn't imagine what it must feel like to learn your entire past is a lie.

I can't speak as I take in this vast, opulent bedroom, the opposite of our airy white-washed cottage. In my mind's eye, I see my mother darting around this room and sleeping in that bed. She's standing beside the wardrobe and reading in front of the fireplace . . . I shake my head, refusing to believe Porter's words.

My mother never spoke about her family, always claiming her mother had died long ago and she'd lost her father soon after. She's never given me any reason to suspect otherwise.

I dig my fingernails into the armchair as bitter rage pours into me. "Liar," I scream.

"I'm not lying, Julietta. Your mother left Aravid at about your age, and with your face so swollen and bruised, Commander Averett mistook you for her." He glances down and lowers his voice, speaking to himself. "My blood runs through her veins, and I wouldn't take my word for it either." He lifts his head and reaches his hand out. "May I see your cloak?"

I'm sitting on most of it and make no move to hand it over. The thought of Porter using something of my mother's to further manipulate me makes me furious.

"Please, child, just look at the clasp. Your mother's name will be engraved on it."

I can't help but glance down at the clasp and lift it up,

running my finger around the crest of the Woodland Realm. My heart jerks as I feel another marking along the edge. It's the smallest script I've ever seen, but it clearly reads *Emilia*.

Clutching a fistful of the cloak, I fight back tears. "You replaced it with another cloak. This one doesn't belong to me," I say through my teeth. "My mother's name is Gwendolyn Lark."

"Gwendolyn was her middle name, and I used to call her my little lark as she was always flitting about," Porter says quietly. "Your mother has never been anything like me. I saw her goodness as weakness, and all throughout her childhood I pushed her away, believing it would make her stronger. I was stubborn, a fool really. I tried too hard to control her. More than anything, I wish I would've based our relationship on who your mother truly was," his voice breaks, "not who I wanted her to be."

I recoil as he leans forward, picking up the wooden box I'd dropped on the floor.

He pulls out the journal and holds it up. "Four years ago, this was sent to me after your cottage caught fire. The flames melted the lock, and I've been too afraid to damage it further by prying it open." He nods toward my cloak and offers me the journal. "We both own one half of a whole, don't we?"

The journal trembles in my hands. Tears fill my eyes as I press the clasp of my mother's cloak against the lock, as I've seen her do a hundred times before. It clicks open.

My tears splash onto the drawing on the first page, onto the folds of skin, delicate eyelashes, and tiny fingers and toes. Under it is my mother's handwriting.

Julietta Gwendolyn Lark, who's given me the sweetest memories I could ever ask for.

A sob builds up deep inside me as clips of memory flash before my eyes.

"I am not worried about Porter finding her body." Madame circles the commander like prey.

"Why not?" he spits out. *"I most certainly am!"*

"Because there is no body," she whispers and slits his throat. *"She's still alive."*

In a blink, I'm beside my mother's bed in the asylum as I read her mind, seeing pictures of gardens in bloom and glittering fountains. Skies flooded with soft clouds and a tangerine sun . . . images that never made any sense until now. Has my mother's coma brought her back to a childhood spent in Aravid?

Porter reaches out to touch my hand, but I jerk away.

Sorrow fills the lines of his face. "Whatever you've heard about me is no longer true. Your mother left a father who created the Maze. She hasn't met the one who regrets it," he says. "I see your mind cannot be read, but can you accept something from me, a memory to prove my words are true?"

I lift my eyes to his, searching for a sign that he's manipulating me.

A tear slips down his cheek before he wipes it away.

This Porter is nothing like the one I saw in that memory. Still, the idea of having his thoughts in my head twists my stomach. But unless I see what he's offering to show me, I'll always wonder if what he's saying is true.

Hesitantly, I take his hand, and his skin tingles beneath my fingertips.

Porter smiles faintly. "It's one of my favorites, but I would like you to have it. No, I need you to have it, Julietta."

Colors rush behind my eyelids as my head fills with the warmth of receiving a new memory . . .

Emilia is so young, so full of life, holding her child in a soft blanket and whispering words too quiet to hear. She lifts Julietta up and kisses both cheeks, her own shiny with tears. Emilia hasn't stopped smiling, looking as if she has finally found that which makes her whole.

The scene trickles into darkness, but my heart threatens to burst with the joy housed in the memory. I want to call it back and never leave the place Porter took me. The images of him as a ruthless ruler and the love threaded throughout that memory collide within my mind.

"Your mother met Greer when he was training to become a commander. We'd hosted a banquet for his regiment here in Aravid," Porter says, sitting in the chair across from me. "Never once had I imagined my Ungifted girl would fall in love with a young Sifter boy. When I refused to sanction their courtship, your father escaped his post in Kripen and your mother left Aravid. They made it all the way to Blare before I caught up with them. You, my dear, were the reason I left well enough alone. I've kept watch ever since the day you were born, but it was my own arrogance that kept me from knowing you."

I drop my head into my hands, unable to fight this swell of emotions any longer.

Up until this moment, I thought I knew everything about my mother. There are so many questions and not nearly enough answers, but the memories of my childhood are already changing. The gaps of my mother's past are filling in, reminding me just how strong she truly is.

My mother, always so soft-spoken and joyful, found the courage to defy a ruler like Porter to fight for the future she longed for.

When Porter places his hand on top of mine, I don't pull away.

"I've wished for this moment since the day I first saw you," Porter says, his voice thick with emotion. "Forgive me that it's taken so long for us to get here."

As I look up at him, I realize it isn't just my mother who broke free from the chains of the past, but her father too. I see his love for us in how he's taken care of her journal and feel it nestled deep in the memory of me. He couldn't fake that, even if he tried.

I push myself onto my feet and wrap my arms around

him. He's shaking, his tears dripping on my hair, as I hug him tighter. It's a while before he stops crying, but there's a strength in his vulnerability, in the way he so openly admits his regrets. As I cry along with him, I'm filled with pride and hope that maybe all the wrong that's happened between him and my mother can truly be made right.

Porter kisses the top of my head. "If I'd known you were in Craewick, I'd have sent my entire army to fetch you. Has Madame held you prisoner?"

With a heavy heart, I explain the past week, about my pledge to the Shadows and how I planned to steal his map of the Maze to free Greer and prevent Madame's coming war upon the Realms. The longer I speak, the paler he becomes, but Porter nods every so often to let me know he's following along. And finally, I tell him about how I betrayed Greer and how my mother fell into her coma by my own doing.

"The nurses aren't sure she'll ever wake up, but she's moving her fingers—" I say.

Porter clasps my hands. "She's coming back, Julietta. In all the coma patients I've seen, the ones who move are close to waking. I'll do everything in my power to ensure she does." He pulls an auction notice from his jacket pocket. "Madame sent me one, as well. It's taken her years to build up an army, and now, she'll do whatever it takes to force my allegiance. She's always sought to wear the only crown."

I gasp as I take the notice. "On the way here, Madame sent Minders to drag me back to Craewick. I always thought she was threatening Mother to punish me . . . that she was going to kill her just to watch me suffer," I whisper. "But we've always been pawns in her game against you, haven't we?"

Porter nods grimly, glancing out the window beside the fireplace. "Even as a child, Madame was cold and distant, but it wasn't until her father's murder that she became paranoid and delusional. Her military counsel was in charge of housing the memories of each prior ruler of the Stone Realm, but she disbanded the counsel to take on all those memories herself. She distanced herself from the other rulers and trusted no one. In return, we distrusted her. Like Bray told you, Madame tried to make herself invincible and has created a thirst for power that nothing can satisfy." He meets my eyes. "Her given name is Clemma, which I'm not sure she even remembers anymore. She was never strong enough to form her own identity and took away the opportunity for her people to form theirs. She uses fear as a weapon, destroying confidence and the ability to think for oneself. For a while, I did the same in Aravid, but the grief of losing you and your mother gave me the strength to break ties with Madame."

I smile sadly, thankful not every event sparked by the accident was bad.

"She believes I'm a recluse now, an opinion I haven't

wanted to change to protect the Aravid people. I feared if she learned too much about how we functioned, she'd exploit our weaknesses. But now I know that by not engaging Madame, I'm somewhat responsible for allowing her to gain control over the Realms," Porter says before the confidence returns to his voice. "But all hope is not lost. Your father, Julietta, lives in the Maze but he's never been a prisoner of mine. He's an ally, to say the least. Many times, Greer wished to send word to Bray that he was alive, but we couldn't risk his whereabouts resurfacing. Though I'm certain he would've searched for you if he knew you were still alive. Madame told him you'd been killed soon after you betrayed him."

A tear slips down my cheek.

Porter clenches his jaw. "Greer always understood that Madame, the vile creature that she is, manipulated you into giving up his location. He never blamed you for what happened. He would've willingly given himself up to save you and your mother."

"I know he would've," I say as my throat closes. "That's what makes the fact that I betrayed him hurt so much."

Porter places his hand on top of my mine. "Madame tried very hard to destroy the only ones who can defeat her now. I'll fight her with every breath I have, and I'm certain Greer will do the same. We're going to win, Julietta."

In the midst of feeling such hope, a shiver runs through me at the determination in Porter's words. I sense an edge within him, one that never dulled with his change of heart. His openness and vulnerability haven't made him weak. Instead, there's power within him which runs deeper than any strength Madame has ever owned. And to her, Porter is the worst kind of enemy—a man who thinks for himself.

He takes the necklace Bray gave me out of his pocket. "This once belonged to my mother, and my grandmother, and my great-grandmother."

Drawing in a long breath, I wipe the tears from my cheeks. "I'd never seen it before Bray gave it to me."

"Mmm. The Minders must've stolen it before setting fire to your cottage. But for once I'm glad they took something that didn't belong to them. It's brought you back to me." He places it around my neck. "I wish you to have it. It's rightfully yours, after all. And if you'll have me, I would love nothing more than to be your grandfather."

I lift his hand and kiss it.

CHAPTER
14

I change my tattered clothes to some I find in my mother's wardrobe. Tears well in my eyes as I stare at myself in the mirror and imagine my mother wearing this deep blue tunic and dark pants. When I wrap her cloak around my shoulders, I can almost feel her here with me, giving me the strength to go on.

The gash on my cheek still hurts, so a servant gives me a healing cream to take the swelling down on my face. It's the color of lavender, smells faintly of violets, and burns and tingles. Seconds later, the pain vanishes and the redness around the cut fades to a soft pink.

Just before I leave the room, I take my mother's auction notice and throw it into the fireplace, watching as the script lights on fire before the letter turns to ash.

Standing beside Porter out in the hallway is a lanky man with wiry white hair sticking out in all directions, his face nearly identical to Porter's. He's wearing a Minder uniform and hops to attention when he spots me.

"Oh, Julietta, how beautiful you are!" he cries before glancing back at Porter. "She looks just like Em, doesn't she, Brother? Just like her, you see!"

Walking toward them, I grin, recognizing his voice from when he rummaged through my mother's room earlier.

Porter chuckles. "Julietta, meet your mother's favorite uncle, Felix."

I laugh as Felix springs forward and wraps his arms around me.

"Being her only uncle, I'll admit there wasn't much competition. But if she'd had a hundred more, I like to believe I'd still hold my place." He draws back and puts his hands on my shoulders. "We had lost hope, but we were wrong to do so. Very wrong, indeed."

My heart swells at the love I hear in his voice. To know I not only have a grandfather but a great-uncle, one who cared so deeply for my mother, makes me long to reunite them all. I glance between the brothers and grin. In less than a week, my family has doubled.

When Felix offers his arm, I loop mine through his. "You're a Minder?" I ask him, glancing at his Gifted tattoo, an eye like Porter's.

186

"Yes, yes. Your grandfather advises our military, of course, but nowadays, he prefers to watch over our people while I oversee the troops here in Aravid."

"Your Minders don't train in Kripen?" I ask.

"Oh, goodness no, my dear. We can do without the tactics of Kripen, thank you very much," Felix scoffs, and I let out a breath, relieved he isn't one of the commanders Madame has been manipulating. "Though to be honest, I never wanted to be a Minder. I'd always hoped to spend my days exploring life outside of the Realms. Your mother and I devoted many hours to discussing where we'd go and who we might meet. Perhaps our dream shall come true one day, but for now, Aravid is where I need to be."

"I've often found the best person to put into power is the one who doesn't want it," Porter says quietly to me.

Felix pats my hand. "I'll retire one day soon, you see. I'm not as young as I look," he says with a wink. "And Porter's even older."

"I'm not sure three minutes counts as *older,* Brother."

Though intimidating from the outside, the inside of Porter's castle is stunning, its own maze of shiny marble floors and curved hallways filled with amber sconces and dozens of mahogany doors. After days of hiking, the plush carpet feels wonderfully cloudlike beneath my boots, and the walls are covered with tapestries woven with hundreds of colorful threads.

We pass through a glass atrium leading to the most

beautiful garden I've ever seen. I can't stop smiling as we go under an archway made entirely of trees, their branches intertwined as if they've been braided. The gardens are a sea of lavender, turquoise, citrusy yellow, and fuchsia spread across a lush green lawn. A light breeze carries a sweet scent from the fields of wildflowers, a mix of honeysuckle and violets, and thick tunnels made of ivy provide much needed shade over the pebbly walkways.

"I've seen this before in my mother's memories. She loved these gardens," I say, stunned by how peaceful a place her mind has chosen. "This is where the coma has kept her."

Porter places his hand on my shoulder. "Your mother spent nearly every day out here with your grandmother. Perhaps her mind is rebuilding itself from the ground up, vines of memory which need time to grow strong before detangling." He plucks a violet and gives it to me. "After years of experimenting, I discovered that violets are not only good for the soul but also for the body. Their petals contain a healing compound, an oil which stimulates the brain to repair itself. It's a long, tedious venture, but if given the time, the results have been close to miraculous. Using this compound, Greer has been rehabilitating those who suffered in the Maze until they're well enough to rejoin my people." He meets my eyes. "I designed the horrors of that prison to destroy their minds. Now it's up to me to piece them back together."

There's shame in Porter's expression, but I sense something greater inside him. He's not dwelling in the past but doing everything he can to help those he hurt.

"I once offered Madame the compound for those in the asylum, but she refused it, of course," Porter says, and it isn't difficult to imagine why. Healing patients would end her thriving treasury. "But now that your mother is moving, I'm certain it will bring her out of the coma."

I let out a cry of joy as I hug him. She's going to come back to us! And never would I have thought her father, Porter of the Woodland Realm, would provide the way.

As I draw back, I see Reid walking down the pathway toward us. A smile spreads across my face as the heaviness in my heart begins to lift.

Felix gives me a gentle nudge. "He hasn't stopped asking about you, my dear."

Wearing a heather gray jacket made from the same Aravid wool as my cloak, he has a black eye from the Minder who knocked him out, but his smile grows as I run toward him. He wraps his arms around me, and I lean my head against his chest, listening to his heartbeat. It's such a beautiful sound that I laugh. To see Reid alive and well fills me up. I didn't even know how empty I'd become. And now that we're back together, I can't bring myself to let him go.

"You're okay," I whisper.

"I was so worried about you," he says at the same time.

Another laugh escapes me. "This isn't exactly how we planned to get that map, but it's turned out a little better, huh?" I draw back to look at him. "Your brother—he's safe, Reid. Porter said everyone in the Maze is thriving."

Tears fill his eyes as he clasps his hands on his head, letting out a long breath. "All this time . . . he's been safe?" Reid grins, looking happier than I've ever seen him.

I hug him once more. After all he's done for me, the only way I could ever thank him is by helping Reid find his brother. To be given the chance to do so now makes me happier than I ever imagined.

Porter and Felix greet him kindly. The shock of the turn of events that we found in Aravid has been slowly wearing off. According to Felix, it took quite a few memories to convince Reid this wasn't some crazy mind game, but now that he knows the truth, he's just as anxious as I am to head for the Maze.

"Even with the map, it won't be easy to get to the Maze. I designed it to be nearly impossible to locate, and I oversaw all prisoner transports just to keep it hidden. Not to mention, if Madame finds you on the way there, she'll use you to force me to stand down when she attacks," Porter says as we sit on benches facing one another.

I glance at Reid. "Reid will make sure we're not tracked by her Minders, and once I have the map, nobody can take it from me. She won't discover our plan."

"But placing you between Madame and me, Julietta—"

"There's no place else I'd rather be," I say.

Porter is silent for a few seconds before giving me a slight nod. "I don't see what other choice we have." He turns to Felix. "Our Minders have grown under your leadership, but we're not strong enough to wage war against Madame."

"But if we do nothing, she'll likely kill Emilia and attack us anyway," Felix answers. "All in three days' time, no less."

"What if you joined forces with the Shadows?" Reid asks. "We have strong numbers and have been crafting weapons for years, but we need allies to win this war. Bray wants Madame knocked off her throne as much as you do."

Felix sits up straighter. "The Shadows would fight alongside our Minders?"

"Bray has already made contact with Sorien in Blare, as well. If everything goes according to plan, we're hoping the Coastal Minders will fight alongside us too." Reid rests his elbows on his knees as he angles toward me. "Do you remember Kellen Marks, Etta?"

"From the auction?"

"Kellen Marks?" Porter and Felix ask at the same time.

"Who is he?" I ask.

"Sorien's nephew," says Felix. "He's been missing for weeks."

"His auction was why I was in Craewick the night

Ryder told me that Etta wanted to meet with Bray," Reid says. "Sorien has been questioning Madame's ideals, to which she retaliated by murdering Kellen. As far as we know, Sorien has no idea what happened to him, so Bray sent a team of Shadows to give him the memories of that night."

I widen my eyes. "That's why Ryder is in Blare?"

Reid nods. "No uncle should have to find out about his nephew's death this way, but it's our only shot at giving Sorien a reason to fight alongside us." He glances between Porter and Felix. "We know Madame has been swaying the loyalty of his commanders to her, but many of them must've known Kellen. Maybe the truth can help break whatever hold Madame has on them. If this doesn't push them over the edge, I'm not sure they'll ever make a move against Madame but we had to try."

"Three allied armies . . . all attacking Craewick?" says Felix, thoughtfully.

"Declan and the Desert Minders will align with Madame, but she won't expect our alliance," says Reid.

"No, I dare say she won't." Porter glances around his gardens. "For years, I've stayed out of her way, but I should've challenged her sooner. Not doing the right thing feels an awful lot like doing the wrong one."

Felix rubs his chin. "I see no reason not to align, but there is one condition I must insist upon. Madame must not be killed."

"Bray's brother was murdered under her orders. He'll kill Madame the first chance he gets," Reid says.

"Then you must convince him not to," Felix says. "Last year, we caught two of Madame's Minders trying to break into Aravid. As I questioned them, I realized there was something wrong with their minds. They were subdued—not their normal, violent selves I saw in their memories. And I sensed a connection which ran to the very core of their beings." He taps his temple. "Madame appears to have a variation of her own. She's figured out how to unite her mind to those of her Minders."

"What?" Reid and I both bark.

"Imagine the majority of Madame's Minders are puppets. They are controlled, submissive. Fully aligned with Madame's consciousness—"

"Like the Minders who attacked me," I say, placing my hand on Reid's arm. "That's why it was difficult for you to get into their heads."

Reid frowns. "Because Madame is already there."

"And if we sever the connection too rapidly, I fear all her Minders will be set loose to wreak all sorts of havoc. Some of them are criminals that Madame forced to the other side of the law through her manipulation. They'll be cruel, unpredictable, untrustworthy, and many will no doubt try to escape Craewick," says Felix. "The timing of our attack will be tricky but if carefully planned, we could subdue enough of them so when Greer takes away Madame's Gift, we can capture the rest and take Madame into custody."

"Not if Bray has anything to say about it," reminds Reid.

"Unless we convince him otherwise," I say, repeating Felix's words.

Reid laughs once. "You know him even better than I do. How well do you think that'll go over?"

"We're fractions of a whole, Reid, each too small to go up against Madame if we don't work together. We have to make Bray see that," I say.

"I think the wisest course would be to attack Craewick as soon as possible, hopefully with the Coastal Minders and the Shadow army as our allies, while you two retrieve Greer," says Felix. "We need to cripple Craewick before Madame summons the troops in Kripen."

"But what will happen to Mother? This attack is what Madame was trying to prevent by sending you that auction notice," I say to Porter.

"It's a thought that also concerns me, but I don't believe any harm will come to her. The very fact that Emilia's in danger will be the reason she's kept alive—her usefulness has not run out. I sent my best scouts to locate her, though I'm sure your mother is heavily guarded and most likely moved from the asylum now," he answers. "That said, we must keep the element of surprise on our side. In case Madame is watching, we'll use the tunnels below Aravid to send out our troops. That's where you and Reid can exit the city, as well."

We all agree that Reid and I should wait until nightfall to leave Aravid, use the cover of darkness to head back to the Mines and present Bray with the alliance. I wish we could go straight to the Maze, but we all know Bray's scouts will never lead one of Porter's men into their compound, especially when Porter is known as a master of manipulation. This information must come from us. Then Bray, Sorien, Porter, and their armies will meet in Craewick.

And when Reid and I arrive with Greer, he'll take away Madame's Gift and end this war before it really begins.

While Porter and Felix instruct their troops, Reid and I walk through the gardens.

"This is where my mother's mind has been the past four years," I tell him as we sit on a bench overlooking a field of violets. "Her coma brought her back to Aravid."

Reid pauses. "What happened the day your mother fell into her coma, Etta? What kind of accident caused it?"

"It wasn't an accident, not really. It was my fault," I whisper, the answer slipping out so quickly that I think I've been ready to tell him for a while now. "A few days before I betrayed the Shadows, Madame sent letters throughout the Realms, claiming to have kidnapped and read a Shadow, and that she'd discovered the identities of a bunch of us. If we didn't return home to face trial, our families would suffer. Do you remember that Shadow I told you about . . . Beau?"

Reid nods.

"Beau was captured by the Minders just before I betrayed Greer. We all knew Madame would see a lot of our faces in his memories, but most of us used nicknames and never discussed where we'd grown up. She had no way of knowing where our families lived. Her letters were just a trap to draw any Shadows stupid enough to believe her lies to come home."

"You were young, Etta, you didn't know," says Reid.

"I should've known! Bray ordered me not to leave the Mines, and I did anyway." I roughly wipe a tear away. "According to that memory that Bray gave me, some commander recognized my mother as Porter's daughter and tipped Madame off, so that's why she was in Blare. Madame was always going to imprison my mother to use as leverage against Porter, but it was my own fault that I showed up too."

I close my eyes as Madame's words rush over me.

I have ensured these events will never be linked to me or you, Commander. No one will ever know you're the one who told me that Porter's daughter was here.

"Just after I got back to Blare, our cottage filled with Minders. There were so many swarming us that I . . . I got confused. I grabbed an arm I thought belonged to a Minder and—" my voice breaks, "I forced every painful memory I could think of into that person. Only it wasn't a Minder. My mother was already in a coma when I realized what I'd done." I take in a shaky breath. "That's when Madame offered me a deal . . . a place for my mother at the asylum if I gave up Greer's location. She even said something about having big plans for me, but I always thought she just wanted to torture me for being a Shadow. Madame knew long before me that I was Porter's granddaughter."

Reid leans toward me, his shoulder pressing up against mine. It's a few seconds before he says, "I blame myself every day for leaving my family, but I can't do anything about it now. And when I find my brother, I won't leave him again. You're going to have a second chance with your mother too."

Tears stream down my cheeks, but something deep inside me swells at his words. For so long, I've carried this secret, the weight of it threatening to crush me each time Reid inched closer to the truth. But like when I told him about Greer, the warmth in his eyes when he looks at me hasn't changed at all.

"How do you do this?" I whisper.

He angles his head. "Do what?"

"Make me feel like anything's possible." I smile at him through my tears before I bite my lip. "Do you remember Kellen Marks' last words?"

"I think everyone in that audience does." Reid inches closer, his fingers brushing across mine. "Better things await me."

"I didn't believe him. So much had gone wrong in my past. I'd lost hope that things could ever be made right." I slip my hand into his and peer up at him. "Meeting you showed me how wrong it was to believe that."

"It wasn't just you who'd lost hope, Etta," he says. "For years I've been so afraid of never finding my brother. Even when you didn't believe it yourself, you showed me how important it is to never stop fighting."

Leaning my head on his shoulder, I close my eyes. Reid wraps his arm around me, and I know this feeling of being so near to him is something I'll never forget. As if nothing in the world can ever harm me.

Reid lets out a quiet laugh. "Only one more day until we find your father and my brother. You're going to love Penn."

CHAPTER

15

"Penn?" The name gets caught in my throat.

For a second, I let myself believe *his* Penn is not the same as *my* Penn, but memories rush through my mind, painting a picture of the similarities between Reid and Penn. There's a peace inside Reid that Penn owned too. I feel the same stability, the same sense of protectiveness, and both have eyes the color of the Blarien Sea that squint when something makes them laugh.

I clutch the edge of the bench as the world spins. Reid says something, but his words don't make any sense. I'm too busy imagining his face when he learns his brother died four years ago.

My heart pounds so quickly that I'm afraid it's going to stop. This front is getting too heavy to hold up. I'm

199

sweating, an icy kind of wetness that invades every inch of me.

Reid sees us as allies now, but what'll happen when he learns I'm the reason he can't save Penn? If we make it to the Maze, he'll find out Penn was never one of Madame's prisoners.

He'll discover I killed his brother.

Reid puts his hand on my shoulder, and I jerk away. "Are you okay?"

Ordering myself to answer him, I open my mouth, but nothing comes out.

"Reid!" Felix rushes toward us from the direction of the castle. "Reid, my boy! Commander Averett and my military counsel need more statistics on the Shadows. Numbers, weapons supply, all that. Can I pull you away for a bit?"

Reid squeezes my hand. "Only one more day until we find your father and my brother," he says with a grin. "I can't believe it."

He turns to wave just before disappearing into one of the turrets, and I can't believe what's happening either. I curse the cleverness of Bray, at how he ensured Reid's loyalty knowing all along Penn is dead.

Reid and I are opponents in a game we're both destined to lose.

"Julietta?"

I angle to the other side of the gardens, where Porter strolls toward the bench.

He sits beside me and gently pats my hand. "Our plan will work, my dear, there's no need for tears. You'll see."

His smile is so genuine that I long to share the truth about why I'm crying. How can I deceive Porter, especially after all he's confessed about his past, about all the mistakes he made with my mother?

"It's not Madame I'm worried about. I've discovered something terrible." As quietly and quickly as I can, I tell him about how my best friend died . . .

His hand clutching my arm, Penn pleads with me to leave Blare and return to the Shadows before Bray discovers we've left.

I glance at my mother, wide-eyed with fear as a group of Minders breaks down the wooden door of our cottage.

Penn yells for me to run, and his hand slips off my arm as a Minder drags him away.

A numbness creeps over my body when Madame steps through the door. She walks toward me, so calmly it looks as if she's floating.

Suddenly, I can't hear Penn's cries or my mother's screams anymore. All I see is the ghost of a smile on Madame's pale lips, how the gold flecks in her eyes burn brighter than fire.

I wait for my heart to stop beating, for her to make me forget how to breathe.

Instead, Madame grabs my arm, her grip as hard as steel around my wrist. "No tattoo. Are you a Shadow, little traitor?" When I don't answer, she yanks me toward her, glancing between my mother and me. "You look just like her." She lets out a laugh before whispering near my ear, "You will not die today. I have big plans for you."

Penn twists from the Minder's grip, swipes a pair of scissors off the table, and plunges them into Madame's back.

With a shriek, Madame lets go, and I jerk away.

I search for pain within my memories, grab the wrist of the closest Minder, and shoot them into his consciousness. It's strong enough to overpower him for a few seconds until he gets the upper hand.

He pushes his own memories of the event that scarred his face into me.

The searing pain of fire climbs up my neck. Screaming, I claw at my throat, trying to extinguish flames that aren't real.

My sight blurs as I force my way back into his mind. There are visions of torture, murder, and auctions. Rage consumes me as I steal them all. But that's not all I'm after.

I snatch the skill I've wanted ever since joining the Shadows—a soldier's fighting talent. My veins tingle with satisfying warmth as the Minder's years of sparring practice dissolves into my every muscle. I've mastered an intricate, lethal dance.

As a Minder drags Penn out the door, I grab my knife and throw it as hard as I can at the soldier's back.

But he spins so quickly that the blade sinks into Penn's stomach instead.

Blood seeps from the corner of Penn's mouth and the look in his eyes is louder than any scream.

I hear and see nothing except for Madame, her eyes glowing

as she twists her head back to me. Her smile only confirms that she manipulated their thoughts. That Minder moved too fast while Penn looked as if he was paralyzed.

Still, I was the one who threw the knife.

Bolting toward him, I shove the Minder's hands off Penn's body. I plead with Penn to stay with me as his head falls into my lap. His eyes flutter open as a crimson stain spreads across his shirt. I trace his face, his skin barely tingling beneath my fingertips.

"I'm sorry," I say between sobs. "I'm so sorry."

"Jules, stop," he whispers. "I love you."

My tears splash onto his face. "And I love you. Always have, always will."

"Never forget me . . . then I'll always be with you."

I cry out as Penn draws his last breath. Light flashes behind my eyes. Searing hot pain slices through my head. When a hand latches onto my shoulder, I promise myself I won't lose another person I love today.

Grabbing her arm, I release the Minder's violent memories into this soldier. I can't see her face clearly through my tears as I gather every painful memory that I own and shove them into my enemy.

I look down when the Minder falls.

Except it isn't a Minder.

Blood drips from my mother's nose. Her bottom lip quivers as she flinches, her chest rising and falling, before going still.

"Mother!" I scream, but her eyes are already turning gray. In

a rush, I read her mind, trying to remove every trace of violence from her memories. But I do it too fast.

Her eyes roll back into her head as she loses consciousness.

As Madame's smile grows, I know what she's thinking. She didn't need to destroy the people I love.

I did it all by myself.

I come back to the present with a shudder.

"None of this would've happened if I wasn't a thief. Greer had rules about never stealing memories just to benefit ourselves, but I didn't care. Once I stole that fighting skill, all I wanted to do was fight. I was blinded by it and look where it got me? My best friend is dead, and my mother is in a coma," I say, fighting back a sob. "And Bray lied to Reid about Penn's death. He's been searching for his brother for years. Years! And Reid has no idea I knew him, let alone . . . oh, Porter, what have I done?"

He pulls me closer, letting me cry. It's a while before I stop, but as he strokes my hair and tells me we'll get through this, I begin to believe him.

"I don't know how to tell Reid the truth," I say, resting my head against his chest.

"Nor do I, Julietta. But is living with the lie any easier? It's clear how much you care for him, but perhaps even clearer how much Reid cares for you," he says softly.

"I wish I was the girl he thinks I am," I whisper.

"What makes you so sure you're not?" Porter lifts my chin with a gentle hand, and I meet his eyes. "The past is a curious thing, isn't it? It's much like these gardens. Once thoughts are planted, they often won't stop growing, especially the things we most regret. That's why we have to cling to the good memories, Julietta. They're what give us springtime in winter. But perhaps there are weeds you need to uproot to let the flowers grow."

His words do little to comfort me. "I don't see many flowers."

"Then you need a better gardener. You don't see the goodness that the rest of us do."

"You're right. I don't see much goodness in this life."

"No, my dear, I meant the goodness the rest of us see in *you*. If I dwelt on my regrets, I wouldn't have the strength to get out of bed every morning. We can't forget what we've done, but it's what we do with those regrets that mold us. We're given a past to learn from and grow, but sometimes the greatest mistake can change a future for the better. And the girl I see sitting before me may have weaknesses but she isn't weak. There's quite a difference." His features soften a bit. "Harness your past and use it for good, Julietta. What is a life without love, or hope and joy? You must live for something higher than yourself. It's who we chose to live *for* that defines us."

Penn's face, bloodied and bruised, haunts me. Who knows what will become of my mother and Greer, or even of Porter and Felix when we go up against Madame.

"What if I lose everyone I love?" I ask.

"Then you must open your heart again. Love isn't always a feeling but a choice, seeking the good of another without expecting anything in return."

His words fill me with an emotion I've so easily forgotten—hope. It's odd to remember how I worried about having his thoughts in my head, terrified they'd prompt me toward evil instead of good. Now I want nothing more than for his way of life to rub off on me.

"Reid deserves to know the truth," I say.

Porter touches my cheek. "Remember, Julietta, always do what is right. The rest will fall into place."

I pace throughout Porter's gardens as I wait for Reid to return from meeting with Felix.

The lanterns strung along the pathways are lit at dusk, the flames flickering in the soft wind. I didn't think it was possible, but it's almost prettier this way. If only I could enjoy it.

Why Bray kept this secret isn't hard to figure out. Reid has been working for him for years, a Sifter capable of collecting more information than any other Shadow. But Bray must've known there was a ticking clock on their alliance when he made Reid and me partners. Once he chose to introduce us, Penn's death could've been revealed at any time.

I collapse on a bench and drop my head into my hands.

Though Bray probably questioned if I'd admit to Reid that I killed his brother, something deep inside tells me Bray already calculated the risk of the truth coming out. And still, he bet everything on the fact that Reid wouldn't seek revenge on me even when it did. This strikes me hard and deep. If he trusts Reid this much, Reid must be as good a guy as he seems.

At the sound of footsteps, I lift my head.

"The Woodland Minders are incredible, Etta. Well-trained, well-armed, and prepared," Reid says, the gold flecks in his eyes shining brighter than ever as he sits beside me. "I only wish there were a thousand more."

"A thousand more, yes," I whisper.

"But if this army aligns with the Shadows, I think we have a shot at winning this war." He digs into his pocket and hands me a vial of purple oil. "Gifts from Felix. A healing compound for you, with specific instructions. Drink it for the mind. Rub it on scrapes and bruises."

Clutching the vial, I stare at the leather pouch he holds up.

"Blinding powder to use against other Sifters. What good is our Gift if we can't see? Your grandfather is a genius. You won't believe all of his inventions . . ."

As Reid rattles on, all I can focus on is the way his hand keeps reaching toward mine.

I close my eyes. A few tears escape down my cheeks.

When I imagine telling him I killed his brother, the courage he instilled in me throughout our journey vanishes. I'm back in Blare with Penn's blood on my hands as the Minders drag my mother's limp body out of our cottage. I'm seconds from striking a deal with Madame. I'm weak, ashamed, and terrified. No different than I feel right now.

"I should find the Maze alone," I blurt out, cutting him off. "You can stay in Aravid."

"Stay in Aravid?" Reid looks confused, and I don't blame him. "Why would I do that?"

"I don't want to have to worry about you too. Porter can send guards with me to the Maze." I hate the way I sound. Childish and arrogant and selfish. "I don't need you anymore."

For a few seconds, he doesn't say anything, just stares at me like I'm insane. Then he sighs and gets on his feet. "Not this again."

"Not what again?" I snap.

He rubs his hand down his face. "I thought we were past this whole 'I don't need anyone' act. Just tell me what's wrong. Look at me, Etta."

I raise my head slightly.

Reid groans and throws his hands in the air. "Where is this coming from? You can tell me, you know. Anything."

Not anything, I want to scream. "I don't need you weighing me down."

"Weighing you down?" His eyes flash. "You need my help."

"No!" I point to myself. "You've always needed *my* help to find your brother."

A muscle in his jaw jerks. "I know why you're doing this."

I stand and rush toward him. "If you only knew what I did, Reid," I say, but he doesn't move away. "I want to believe I've changed! That I would never betray anyone again after what I did to Greer, but I'm exactly the same."

"Not true." He draws closer, and I step back. "You haven't betrayed me."

His words are so soft and kind, and it's the worst thing he could've said. "Run as far away from me as you can," I say.

"I'm not the one running. Don't you understand why you're doing this?"

"If you have all the answers, then just tell me!" I cried.

Before I can turn away, Reid cups my face in his hands.

I order myself to run, to find a way to forget the past three days ever happened. But I draw closer as he leans in, pressing his lips against mine. Our kiss is so light, so soft, that when he pulls back, I wonder if it happened, but my lips gently tingle. Reid's mind was open to me. How much does he trust me to do that?

He rests his forehead on mine. "If you admit you care about me, I'm one more person you're afraid to lose. You're terrified, but you keep coming closer. There's no reason to pull away."

In this moment, I want nothing more than to fade into him. To lean my head against his chest and let him hold me, but there's every reason to pull away. I can't let him risk his life to protect me without knowing the truth.

As difficult as it is to leave Reid, I return to the bench, afraid if I don't give my fingers something to hold, I'll flee. He's become a part of my past. Another goodbye.

"Be honest with me, Etta. Please," he says, sitting beside me.

Taking in a breath, I push my panic down. "When I left the Shadows, I didn't realize he'd followed me until we hit the outskirts of Blare—"

"Who? Bray?"

"No . . . my partner." I meet Reid's stare, knowing this is the last time he'll look at me as his friend. "Penn."

His lips part slightly. "Penn?"

I hear so much in his brother's name—shock, sadness, regret, confusion. Admitting I knew Penn hits me so hard that I can only imagine how Reid is feeling. "Penn told me he had an older brother, but Greer didn't let us use names whenever we spoke of our families in case one of us was ever read by the Minders," I whisper. "When they attacked us in Blare, I . . . I couldn't save him."

"No." His voice breaks. "He's in the Maze. Penn is—"

I shake my head.

"But he was Ungifted. He couldn't have been a Shadow!"

"He must've discovered his Gift after you left the Tribes." Tears spill down my face as I slip off my bracelet and place it between us, the embossed *P* exposed. "Penn was my best friend."

Instinctively, I put my hand on his forearm and feel a rush of energy leave my body.

Reid stands so quickly that I recoil. His face changes from disbelief, to rage, to sorrow when tears flood his eyes.

My skin tingles with the warmth of using my Gift, and I'm shaking as I realize I've accidentally given him a memory. I frantically sift through my thoughts for whatever was at the forefront of my mind when Reid says, "You . . . you killed him. Your mother's coma . . . my brother . . . oh, Etta, what have you done?" he cries. "He was only trying to protect you!"

"I didn't mean to give you that. I didn't mean to," I say, my words rushing out as the images of Penn's death fill my mind. I cry out when I realize I've given Reid the memory and yet, I still have it too.

A deep, powerful ache blooms in my chest as I watch him reliving my memory, the emotions I felt the day Penn died flooding him so rapidly that he covers his face with his forearm, his shoulders heaving up and down.

"I'm so sorry," I say between sobs. "I wish I'd died instead of him."

When he lifts his head, I can tell by his expression

211

that Reid now sees me for what I truly am—his brother's killer. His eyes are bloodshot as he draws so close that I lean back.

Reid puts his finger under my chin, forcing me to look at him. "This journey was never about saving your mother's life." His whisper is rough and deep, the gold flecks in his eyes like glowing embers. "It was about making sure you aren't her murderer too."

As he walks away, I call out his name until he disappears out of the gardens. Once he's gone I stop trying to be strong. Stop pretending things will be made right. Anger comes first, a sickening wave of fury. I scream and clutch Penn's bracelet in my fist. Then I bury my face in my hands and cry.

16

Commander Averett and I leave Aravid as soon as the sun sets. My eyelids are heavy, and my body aches from all this traveling, but with only two days until the auction, there's no time to slow down.

Saying goodbye to Porter and Felix was more difficult than I imagined. Having only just met them, the deep worry I felt in knowing they'd soon be in battle had surprised me. They've stamped themselves on my heart.

After observing the Woodland Minders and spending what little time we found together, I'm confident they have a chance at taking over Craewick. If Bray sides with them, maybe we really can turn these odds against Madame. But we all know our greatest hope still lies with Greer.

"This map is meant for a Sifter's mind," Porter had warned before we set out. "There's a lot of energy attached."

I'd nodded. Sifters don't get headaches and fevers, their minds capable of holding more energy than ours, but I've always been able to handle large amounts of foreign memories without feeling ill. When I mentioned this to Porter, he said, "Hmm. Well, you do have quite a few Sifters in your ancestry," before I clasped his hand.

Staring at the map spread across my desk, I smile at the intricacies of my design. I scan over every detail, chart every course from each Realm straight to its entrance. It's well-hidden, marvelously constructed. A work unrivaled by any Sifter before me and perhaps any after.

I shut my eyes, making certain the memory is engrained upon my mind.

Then I roll up the map, throw it into the fire, and watch it burn.

Blinking, I pulled out of Porter's consciousness, bracing myself for the side effects that should inevitably come from holding this memory. There was no pulsing behind my eyelids. No blurred vision or a headache.

"I have it," I told him, sensing how proud he was of designing the Maze. Pride swelled up inside me too as the memory manipulated my emotions. "And I feel fine."

"Good. You must be quick to find it, my dear. I have no doubt Madame's scouts are watching Aravid, but the darkness should help keep you hidden. And Commander Averett, of course, will keep you safe." Porter gave me a tired smile and held my shaking hands. "Remember, child, being brave doesn't mean you aren't afraid of anything. Just that fear doesn't stop you from fighting for something you believe in."

I rose up on my tiptoes and kissed his cheek.

Commander Averett and I take the underground tunnels to a set of stone stairs leading up into the forest. With the shortcuts Felix suggested, we should reach the Mines by tomorrow afternoon at the latest, but my heart aches as I imagine returning without Reid.

Moonlight peeks through the pines, bathing the woodlands in a shimmery light. In the still of the forest, my memories speak to me once again. They sneer and bite like Madame's bloodthirsty hounds.

Over and over again, I hear Joss's pleas not to leave the Shadows. I see Cade frantically searching the tunnels of the Mines, looking for me. I feel Penn's lifeless hand within mine.

Then I imagine Reid's face when I gave him the memory of his brother's death.

As the sun rises above the treetops, our path ends at a nest of boulders. Behind it is a wall of smooth gray rock rising up as far as I can see. We can go right or left, and I know from Reid's memory of the Mines' location that it's a left.

Commander Averett puts her hand on my arm. "Let's rest, Julietta. Your face is flushed, and you can barely put one foot in front of the other. The map could be playing with your mind."

Dragging myself over to the rock wall, I swing my pack off and sit against it. I let her believe it's the map giving me all these problems, though my head feels fine. I just don't want to reveal that all night I've done nothing but relive my time with Reid. Though like with Cade, Joss, and Penn, the memories are tainted with sadness because now I know how our story was always going to end.

Commander Averett sits beside me, and I lean my head back to watch the sunrise.

"Do you have a family, Commander?" I ask her.

"A man I love more than life itself and three copies of him."

"All boys, huh?"

"They're a handful but I wouldn't have it any other way. Your mother was one of the few who could keep up with them, and they loved her for it," she says. "Emilia is a beautiful person, a lot like your grandmother."

I angled toward her. "You knew my grandmother too?"

"I've known your family as long as I've known my own. I have many stories when we find the time." Pulling a rag from her pack, she cleans the blade of her knife with smooth, steady strokes. "We're in very good hands,

Julietta. Your grandfather is the best strategist I've ever encountered, and Felix is one of the toughest, cleverest commanders I've ever served."

I laugh. "Felix, tough?"

She winks at me. "Some don't need to flex their muscles to prove their strength."

The back of my neck tingles.

Just like with Madame's Minders, there's no one there, and when I blink, Reid is standing right before us. He's trembling from head-to-toe, uncontrolled in a way I've never seen from him before. With his clenched jaw and red-rimmed eyes, Reid looks like a stranger.

For a moment, I freeze. The edges of my vision darken, leaving only him. It's the first time since we've met that the only emotion I feel toward Reid is fear.

Beside me, Commander Averett lifts her knife.

I'm lightheaded as I push myself to my feet and step between them.

Reid eyes me so intensely I don't move any closer.

When his focus shifts to Commander Averett, I say, "Commander, please, lower your weapon."

"I have orders to protect you," she says under her breath.

"Your Gifts are equally matched, and he can fight as well as anyone in your army," I whisper over my shoulder. "That knife won't do anything except put him more on edge."

Reid moves toward us, and a shiver runs down my spine at the coldness in his stare. "You know what I realized halfway out of Aravid? You're the only one who knows the way back to the Mines."

I frown. "Why go back? There's nothing left for you there."

"Nothing left for me?" he spits out. "For three years, I worked for Bray. For three years, he let me believe I could save Penn! He swore to protect the Shadows, but what if it's all a lie? If his only goal is killing Madame, then he doesn't care who lives and who dies. I won't abandon all those kids to suffer because of him."

I shudder at the thought of Reid confronting Bray. Pitting Sifters against one another never ends well. "If we don't all work together, the Shadows are going to suffer anyway," I tell him as calmly as I can. "I hate that Bray lied to you, but he's our only shot at getting our armies to work together. The Shadows follow Bray. They *trust* him." I step closer. "I can't ever tell you how sorry I am for what happened to Penn, but I'm the one who hurt your brother, not Bray."

Tears stream down his face before he groans, turning his back on us.

My throat closes as I watch him cry. I know exactly how he feels. Like his only job in the world was to protect Penn and he failed.

I turn to face Commander Averett. "You need to go back to Aravid."

"My job is to protect you," she repeats, planting her feet.

I lower my voice to a whisper. "Staying here isn't the way to do that. Porter needs to know Bray and Reid are fighting their own battle against one another. If I'm forced to take him back to the Mines, let me try to convince Reid that we all need to work together." I grab her pack and shove it into her hands. "He isn't going to hurt me."

Even as they fly out of my mouth, I doubt my own words. But Reid chose to trust me when he couldn't be certain that I wouldn't hurt him in some way. And in this moment, I'm choosing to do the same.

Commander Averett glances between Reid and me before giving a brief nod. "I'll never forgive myself if something happens to you, but I'll get the message to Porter. I swear it." Putting on her pack, she gives Reid a harsh look before disappearing into the woods.

When I turn back around, Reid's already looking at me. His eyes are dark and distant, his jaw rigid and set.

"I'm so sorry," I say quietly. "I don't know what else to say."

In his silence, there are so many things I want to explain, to make him understand that if I'd only known what awaited us in Blare, I never would've gone back. I keep quiet, knowing my words will fall on deaf ears. For four years I lived with the guilt of Penn's death, unable to believe things could ever be made right. If it's taken me that long to start to forgive myself, how can I ever expect Reid to forgive me now?

"Take me to the Mines," Reid says through his teeth. "Now."

I force myself to meet his stare. "I'm begging you to help the Shadows win this war. If we can't stop Madame, she'll hunt the Tribes—" I stop speaking as his face hardens. "It isn't the time to confront Bray."

He strides toward me. "After all this, you're worried about what happens to Bray?"

"To *Bray*?" I slam my hands into his chest, pushing him away as rage overpowers my fear. "I'm not worried about Bray! I'm worried about you!" I point to myself, unable to stop my tears. "I know what it's like to take a life. And once you cross that line, there's no coming back."

"The Shadows deserve a better leader than him!"

"We all deserve a better leader than one who builds their throne on murder," I hiss before turning my back toward him, the fight leaving me just as quickly as it came. "But if you want revenge, you've already found me."

I close my eyes as he draws close behind me.

"You may have been lying about who you were, but I never lied about who I was. My family means everything to me," he says, his breath warm on my neck. "You're the only one who can free Greer, and Greer is the only one who can stop Madame. I won't let you be the reason I lose more people I love."

My body feels cold and limp at his words. The truth in them slices through me, splitting open wounds that had begun to heal in Aravid.

As I force myself to move toward the Mines, I fight to remember the hope I found in Porter's gardens. If someone like Porter can leave his past behind, I thought maybe one day I could too. But with each silent hour that passes between Reid and me, our time in Aravid slips further and further away. As much as I want to believe Porter's words that a heart can heal, mine feels as if it's shattered.

Using the shortcuts Felix suggested, we knock off nearly a day of traveling, and the sun is still high as we approach a trapdoor into the Mines. Reid follows so closely that I feel the energy radiating off his skin as I spot a scout high in a tree. The second she sees Reid, she lowers her bow and vanishes into the leaves.

Brushing past me, Reid pops the latch open and heads down the ladder without a word.

We twist through the tunnels to the cavern which holds the memory market. The booths are nearly deserted. Most have been stripped clean, all those supplies now with the Shadows standing in large groups.

A few glance over at Reid, but quickly return to whatever they're doing when he ignores them. Many carry bows and arrows on their backs with sharp blades on their hips as they listen to various leaders calling out orders.

Protect the Ungifted. Kill the Minders. I take in a long breath. The auction is the day after tomorrow, so we barely have time to meet with Bray and head out again. We'll need to be in the Maze by tomorrow morning if we have any hope of being back in Craewick by Auction Day.

Across the cavern near the armory, Bray meets my eyes and strides over to meet us.

Reid clenches his hands into fists, and I curse myself for not putting up more of a fight to avoid bringing him back.

It's clear from the hard lines of his face that Bray thinks we failed in Aravid. Before he can ask, I say, "I have the map, but there's more you need to know." I glance around at the Shadows watching us, afraid I've already said too much. If any one of them has their mind read during battle, it could tip Madame off to our plan. "We need to talk alone."

We follow Bray down the tunnels to the dungeons. There are prisoners screaming behind locked doors, and I wonder how many of them are Madame's soldiers, their minds being manipulated as they try to claw their way out of these cells.

"What happened in Aravid?" Bray says as we enter an empty cell far away from the other prisoners, his eyes flickering to Reid.

Trying to keep the focus off Reid, I tell Bray as quickly as I can about our journey, giving just enough detail to foster an alliance with the Woodland Realm and make him understand it's our only option. His eyes go wide when I tell him about Porter being my grandfather but get very narrow when I share about Madame's deep control of the Minders and the kind of violence they'll unleash if he kills her.

"Neither you nor Porter have the numbers to win this war, but together, we have a fighting chance against Madame. And since Porter will align with you—" I say.

"But only if Madame lives, right?" Bray says flatly.

"Her Minders are criminals, Bray. Dangerous, violent, unpredictable. There has to be time to subdue them. Allying with Porter is what's best for the Shadows."

"Do you want to know what's best for the Shadows? Madame, dead and buried," he hisses. "Porter is manipulating you, Jules. Whatever was inside his memory of the Maze has clouded your judgment. What happens when I reveal my entire army to that madman? He'll destroy us."

"No, he won't!" I hold my hand out. "I'll give you a memory to prove it."

"There's no way I'm letting you inside my mind," he snaps.

"Everything she said is true," Reid says in a low voice.

Bray crosses his arms and drills his sight into Reid. "Look who's finally decided to chime in. What was the point of sending you to Aravid if you couldn't even keep Porter from manipulating her? She's completely useless now."

That's all it takes for Reid to come toward him.

I close my eyes. "Reid, don't do this."

"Do what?" says Bray. "If you've got something to say, just say it, Reid."

Reid shoves a finger in his direction. "You knew. This whole time, you *knew*. What kind of twisted person uses someone's dead brother to earn loyalty?"

"The kind that knows losing a brother is the worst kind of pain someone can know," he says, not missing a beat. "Saving Penn was what drove you."

"Then I should be thanking you?" he spits out.

"No, but I'm not the one who killed him," Bray says coldly, looking at me. "Want to know who did?"

"I already know who did! At least Etta was honest with me," Reid shouts. "But you? You *use* people. You manipulate because you're not a good enough leader to earn trust yourself. You're no different than Madame, don't you get that?"

When Bray lunges at Reid, I jump between them.

Bray whips the back of his hand across my face so hard I stumble and fall. I cry out, though I barely feel the hit. What stings deeper is the realization that the Bray I once knew, whose arms were always there to catch me when I fell, is nothing like the one standing before me.

Reid charges, slamming Bray into the wall. Reid lands a punch across his jaw before Bray drives his knee into Reid's stomach. Reid's knees hit the ground, and

Bray kicks him in the chest and whips the knife off Reid's belt.

"Stop!" I say.

Jerking Reid to his feet, Bray wraps his arm around his neck, the blade at Reid's throat.

My fighting skill flares up, my veins tingling with warmth. Every bit of me wants to attack Bray, but I force myself to remain still as he tightens his grip on the hilt of the knife.

"Killing Madame will never bring Cade back, but we can still defeat her if you align with Porter. This isn't any different than your plan," I say.

"Aligning with Porter was not my plan," Bray yells. "He sat back and did nothing while Madame murdered innocents year after year. Porter isn't my ally, and if you can't see that then you aren't mine either." He jerks his head toward the shackles at the back of the cell. "Lock yourself up."

"No, we have to free Greer! You have to let us go." I scream again when the tip of the knife draws blood on Reid's neck. "This is between you and me, Bray. It has nothing to do with him!"

"You forget how well I know you, Jules. Torturing him hurts you more than I ever could. Now lock yourself up." Bray's voice is as low as a growl. "You're both staying here until this is all over."

Reid's eyes are slits, swollen and red. He couldn't fight

Bray with his Gift even if he tried. He blinks twice, eyeing the small pouch hanging from his belt.

My heart races at the sight of the blinding powder, his keepsake from Felix.

Reid nods once just before jamming his elbow into Bray's stomach.

Bray cowers before raking the knife across Reid's back.

Reid rears up, a look of anguish on his face, as I crash into Bray.

He loses his footing, slamming into the wall behind us before he throws me off him.

Then the cell fills with chalky gray dust.

The blinding powder burns like fire on my skin, but I've turned quickly enough to keep it out of my eyes.

Bray falls to his knees beside me, his pupils already glazed over.

I bolt toward Reid and swing his arm across my shoulders, but he pushes me away.

"Get out of here, Etta," he yells.

"Quiet!" I clutch him as hard as I can, dragging him out of the cell. I slam the door behind us and lock it with the steel lever. It rattles on its hinges as Bray pounds on it, and we stumble down the hallway.

"I can't see anything." Reid grimaces, his eyes gray and lifeless. "Just go. I'll only slow you down."

Staring at the crimson cut down his back, I snap, "You really think I'm going to leave you here?"

I wrap my arm around his waist as he leans on me, and I search for an exit through the narrow tunnels. We finally come across a trapdoor which leads out into the forest.

Reid's eyes shine like glass in the sunlight before he leans over and coughs. His sleeve comes away bloody.

Clenching my hands into fists, I realize any fear I felt toward Reid has vanished. He hasn't stopped looking at me like I've betrayed him, but defending me against Bray proves he's not going to hurt me. All I feel now is fury at what Bray has done to him.

I yank him along between the trees and as we wade through streams to cover our tracks. I'm terrified that the scouts surrounding the Mines will start after us, but no one comes down from their perches in the trees. Not without orders from Bray.

As if reading my mind, Reid says, "Bray will send scouts—"

"Bray's locked in the dungeon. We still have time to get away from here," I say.

"Head starts don't matter with good scouts and limping runaways. I'm slowing you down."

"What do you want from me? To apologize because I didn't let you die back there?" I clutch him tighter. "Just keep moving!"

Pulling up the map of the Maze in my memories, I recall what Porter said just before I took it . . .

"The northern route into the Maze is longer but infinitely safer."

"But if another route is faster—" I say.

"No, Julietta, the entrance is on the edge of Kripen's training fields. And that section of the Maze is no longer used. Greer and the others reside in the heart of the prison, but the outskirts are filled with traps and obstacles that were too dangerous to dismantle. Stay away from there. You won't be any help to Greer if you're hurt along the way."

I bite my lip, sorting through our options. It's difficult to imagine anything much worse than traveling through Kripen in broad daylight—except traveling through Kripen in broad daylight while dragging along a blind Sifter. We better hope that Felix's estimated time for this stuff to wear off—"One to two hours, my boy!"—is correct.

"I know where to go. Don't worry," I tell Reid. *But we're going to need that sight of yours to return before we get there,* I almost add.

We zigzag until we hit a large rocky hill that I have to help Reid down. That's when he says, "Wait a second . . . I can feel the sun behind us. Are we heading east?"

When I hesitate, he repeats the question with a harder edge to his tone. "Possibly," I force out.

"East? Toward Kripen?" Reid plants his feet, surprisingly strong enough that I can't move him. "Why?"

"Because we're going to cut through the military base to get to the Maze," I say as if it's the most normal thing in the world.

Reid lets out an angry laugh. "Do you know anything about Minder training? The commanders set criminals loose to hunt them like wild animals—"

"We've got to risk it if we want to be back in Craewick on time." When he still doesn't move, I add, "Do you want to take the lead? Go right ahead! If not, then just calm down."

He doesn't justify that with an answer.

It's a long, tedious hike to Kripen. I wish I could say I'm the picture of courage, but at the sound of each breaking branch or bird that whistles, I'm convinced we're seconds away from the Shadows' ambush to haul us back to Bray. Sweat trickles down my spine. My chest tightens so I can barely breathe.

The one positive is Reid's sight is coming back. He's still pale and trembling, obviously trying to hide his pain. The cut on his back has stopped bleeding, but his knees buckle with each step.

"Let's rest," I say.

"We can't," he says through gritted teeth.

"Five minutes. You're heavy."

Passing this off like I need it more than he does seems to work, and we find a cluster of rocks to sit on. I wish I had something to give Reid to eat. Though judging by the greenish hue of his face, I'm not sure it would help.

"Oh! My gift from Felix," I say, irritated I've forgotten about the vial in my pack. "Drink it."

He pours a drop onto his tongue.

"Take more," I say.

"No, we have to make that last." He sighs and rubs his face. "Good try, but I know we're not resting for you. I'm fine."

I shake my head. "I can't believe Bray did this to you. He's never come close to hitting me before, but I should've known how cruel he'd be if you confronted him." I pause as my memories flare up, reminding me of something that I always wished I'd never seen. "One time, Cade got into a fight with a Hollow who almost killed him. What Bray did to that man . . . it was terrible. I'd never seen him act like that."

"Like what?" Reid asks between hard breaths.

"Like a Minder." I meet his eyes. "I was on scout duty when I came across a man tied to a tree near the Mines. He was so beaten up that I didn't recognize him, but he was wearing the same jacket as when he'd attacked Cade. He tried to say something but choked on his own blood. Suffocated before I could cut him loose. I didn't believe there was much of a difference between justice and revenge before then, but no one should have to die like that."

Reid keeps my gaze until I glance down, my stomach twisting at how beaten and bruised he is.

231

After Cade was killed, the memory of that Hollow became a warning to me. I'd never expect Bray to take his brother's death lightly, but I'd seen what could break him. What has now consumed and destroyed him.

It's dusk when we reach Kripen's borders.

The trees are sparse, the landscape gradually changing from forest to desert. We hide in between a cluster of bushes with gnarled branches to rest for the night. Porter was clever to build the Maze here, where no one visits without a death wish. I dread the thought of what lies ahead for us tomorrow.

Though it's tempting to want to plough through Kripen and get this whole thing behind us, the darkness has a positive and a negative. It might keep Minders from spotting us, but Reid has to see his enemies to use his Gift.

"I should bandage the cut on your back," I tell Reid. "Make sure it doesn't get infected."

Without a word, he lies down on his stomach.

I stifle a gasp when I see the shape he's in. A few of his ribs are broken, the reason why he winces with every breath. There's a ton of dried blood around the gash running down his spine. His body trembles as I dab the cut with the violet compound. I wrap a bandage around him, realizing his skin isn't tingling.

It's a stupid thing to notice at a time like this, but his guard is up. A reminder of how differently his skin felt when he trusted me. How his lips felt when they met mine. But after learning about Penn, how could he ever open up to me again?

Once I'm finished, Reid falls asleep almost instantly, his breathing deep and steady.

I stare at him, my mind flashing with memories. All the harsh words between us in the Mines. Late night talks in the cave. Meeting my grandfather for the first time. But I'll never forget the look of regret that he let himself get close to me. He can feed off the hate for a while. Maybe it'll lessen the hurt. But for me, some of the biggest moments of my life have happened with Reid, a boy I didn't even know existed until four days ago.

A flicker of courage finds its way inside me as Porter's words float through my mind.

Harness your past and use it for good, Julietta. What is a life without love, or hope and joy? You must live for something higher than yourself. It's who we choose to live for that defines us.

Wrapping my cloak tighter around me, I touch Penn's bracelet on my wrist. "I couldn't save you, but I won't let anything happen to your brother," I whisper. "I promise you that."

CHAPTER
18

I wake Reid as the first rays of light appear in the east.

All night, I haven't stopped thinking of Porter, Felix, and the Woodland army. Were they able to leave Aravid without alerting Madame's scouts? Use the element of surprise to attack her? Without help from the Shadows, do we even have a chance to win this war? I almost break down as I picture my mother, defenseless and frail as a battle erupts around her.

I'm shaking as I kneel in front of Reid and dab the compound around his eyes. Thankfully, the swelling has gone down, and the cut on his back isn't getting infected. Though I'm trying to be gentle, Reid's muscles tense beneath my fingers as I redress it. I can't help but think it's not from the pain, but because I'm the one touching him.

Blinking back tears, I push myself to my feet and hold my hand out to Reid.

"We won't last five minutes against the Minders if I can't stand on my own." He grimaces as he rises and takes an unsteady step. "If something happens to me, just keep going." When I don't answer, he adds, "Etta, I mean it—"

I raise my eyebrows. "Or you'll do what?"

"I won't go." Reid angles his head and leans against a tree. "Swear you'll keep going, or I'm staying right here."

"Right here! At the center of Minder territory?" I hiss.

Reid points at the ground. "Right here. Can't have me weighing you down."

"Don't throw my words back at me. You know I didn't mean that!" I will myself to not look away before he does, but I break first and swing my pack on. "Have it your way, Reid."

"And all this time I thought you were a good liar."

"Fine! I'll just abandon you among criminals and Minders," I say, knotting my hair into a bun to get it out of my face. "You're impossible, you know that?"

"*I'm* impossible?" he says, brushing past me.

We have Porter's map to guide us, but even the *correct* route is a nightmare. The sun beats down as we pass between spindly trees and bushes made of prickly thorns. The trail is pockmarked with deadfalls and huge craters filled with jagged rocks.

Hours into our journey, Reid is so exhausted that he keeps tripping on the gnarled vines covering the ground. I grab his arm to steady him, but he jerks away. He falls over and over again, his breathing labored and rough as he pushes himself back to his feet.

Part of me feels horrible that I couldn't protect Reid from Bray. The other half wants to slap him for refusing my help now that we're in this mess.

Reid's face takes on a waxy look, his forehead slick with sweat. I'm terrified he's going to pass out. When we finally come across a tiny stream, I make him pour water over his head to get his fever down.

"Just drink the compound," I snap.

"Quit asking me to do that," he shouts back. "I'm not taking any more. You'll thank me if something happens to you."

I plant my feet and cross my arms. "I'm staying right here until you drink it."

"Don't be stupid, Etta."

"You're the one who taught me how to play this game," I say, holding the vial out to him.

We stare one another down before he mutters something under his breath and tips back the rest of the compound.

Minutes later, the trees have all but disappeared. Up ahead there's a drop-off. My heart pounds as we walk toward it. I instinctively swing my bow off my back, readying to nock an arrow as I finally see what Porter was so worried about.

It's dead silent except for the waves of the Blarien Sea splashing far in the distance. All the way to the beach is wide-open desert. Apart from a few gnarled, scruffy bushes, there's nowhere to take cover. There are steep sand dunes around us, behind which any number of Minders could be hiding.

I squint, spying the sea caves jutting out from the beach. One houses a hidden entrance into the Maze. I suck in a breath as I spot the one from Porter's map and can't help but smile. If we can only get past this last obstacle, we'll find Greer.

"It's that cave," I say, lifting my finger to point it out.

Reid pushes my hand down. "Don't tell me."

"But if we're separated, you should know where to go."

"No. This is why you're carrying that map in the first place. I won't risk giving up that information to the Minders if something happens to me—"

"Stop saying that," I growl.

Reid grabs the collar of my cloak and turns me around to look at him, his grip much stronger than it was before he drank the compound. "Listen to me. No matter what, don't stop running." His eyes narrow, and my mouth dries up. "Swear it."

I glance at the sea caves once again.

I'm ready to face my father. I'm ready for my mother to wake. I'm ready for a new Craewick to emerge from Madame's ashes. But I'm not ready to lose Reid. Promise or no promise, if something happens, I won't leave him. Not when I know Reid's safety is what Penn would want. But I'm a better liar than he gives me credit for.

"I won't stop," I say, and this time, he seems to believe me.

Taking the lead, I emerge from the cover of the last scraggly tree and walk sideways down the steep sand dune. Totally exposed. My pulse rushes as I brace myself for the Minders' attack. Will they shoot us with arrows? Or use throwing knives or flying razors?

The wind picks up, blowing sand as sharp as glass into my face just before something clips my ear.

An arrow sinks into the sand near my boot.

Blood dripping down my neck, I whip around and loose an arrow at the top of a sand dune.

The Minder who shot at me cries out, my arrow lodged in his shoulder as Reid shouts, "Run!"

I blink, and there are Minders crawling all over the tops of the sand dunes. Some are throwing knives while others pelt us with rocks. A stone slams into the side of my face, barely missing my eye. I groan, shooting an arrow into the leg of the first Minder I see. That's when the commanders start calling out tips.

"Little low, soldier! Higher next time, come on!"

"Aim for an eye, but the head will get the job done!"

"Watch 'em twist and turn! They'll slow around the corners. Good time to shoot!"

I up my pace, leading this way and that, following Porter's map until we're forced to slow down because of the wide ravines on the trail. The sand is high on either side, trapping us as we trudge through mud.

"Faster!" says Reid, so close I feel his breath on my neck.

Gritting my teeth, I pull myself up onto dry land.

Up ahead Minders are sliding down the dunes, sand billowing up all around them.

Reid spins around, his back pressed against mine. He's trembling as he knocks out as many as he can using his Gift, but their numbers only multiply as they close in. Heat radiates from his skin. He's too weak to use his Gift this rapidly without damaging his mind.

I shoot an arrow into a pack of Minders before I reach for my last one.

As he goes for the knife on his belt, Reid's hand grazes mine.

I'm certain he didn't mean to touch me, but then he laces his fingers through mine. And in the midst of all of this, the tiniest smile flickers across my face before he lets go.

Nocking an arrow, I raise my bow to shoot the Minder closest to me, but he collapses before I fire.

The soldier behind him drops to the ground, an arrow in his shoulder.

My blood rushes to my ears.

As soon as they realize they're under attack from behind, the Minders charging me whip around, their weapons pointed toward the tops of the sand dunes.

I check on Reid. The Minders rushing him are being picked off one-by-one, but Reid hasn't moved a muscle.

The sun blinds me as I search the dunes for whoever's helping us. My chest tightens as a terrible thought hits me. Have the Shadows found us? Under orders to keep us alive so they can drag us back to Bray?

A Hunter emerges from the tree line.

I gasp when I meet his stare. There's a pack with him, all firing at the Minders with incredible accuracy. A surprised laugh escapes me as I realize it's the Hunter whose friend I saved outside of Aravid, and I raise my hand.

Still wearing the wolf skull, he lowers his bow and dips his head.

When he smiles, I see his teeth are whittled into sharp points, and a chill runs down my spine.

"Move, Etta!" shouts Reid.

As the trail cuts between two high banks of sand, knotted branches form a crude tunnel above our heads. We sprint up a sand dune and stumble down to the beach. The sand is dry and thick, just as difficult to run on as the muddy trails.

I wrap my arm around Reid's waist as we race toward the massive gray cave jutting into the sea. He's breathing hard, his bandages bloody from cuts that've reopened. His skin is as hot as fire.

"Stay close," I say as we wade in, waves crashing against our waists. "With your cut—"

As if on cue, salt water splashes onto Reid's back and he hisses in pain.

"And watch out for riptides," I shout over the waves.

I dive in, swimming beneath the wake until I glide to the top. Reid's close, but grimacing each time he moves. I fight against the current to get to him, terrified he's going to pass out.

In front of the cave's entrance, the current picks us up, slamming Reid against the rocky wall with a loud *crack,* and shooting me into the cave.

Sucking in a breath, I swim under the surface, salt water burning my eyes as I spot him. I grab his waist and kick as hard as I can to the top. My mouth fills with seawater as I scream his name, but he doesn't stir. I drag him into the current, letting it carry us to the beach inside the cave.

My legs cramp as I pull him onto the black sandy shore. I pound my fists on his chest. "Come on, Reid," I say. "Come on!" Then I press my lips to his, breathing for him.

Colors flash behind my eyes.

I draw back at the ripple of memory, at how Reid's skin tingles. In his unconscious state, in my hurry to help him, I've stolen whatever he was just thinking about. Once I see what it is, I'm not sure I want to give it back. It's the moment where his hand found mine during the Minders' attack . . .

We're surrounded on all sides. These Minders are idiots who can barely shoot, but they're idiots with strong numbers. Etta's almost out of arrows. She's trembling but I don't want her to be afraid. I reach for her hand. I'll do whatever it takes to get out of here and let her find her father.

But I might not have the chance to tell her Penn's death wasn't her fault. That memory showed me she loved him as much as he loved her, and I understand why.

These past five days, I've seen a girl who owns the kind of strength that can never be bought. And if I never get to say it, I hope she knows that I wish I did.

"Reid," I whisper, pulling out of the memory as I hit his chest. "Come back!"

He rears up and hunches over, throwing up seawater onto the sand and coughing in fits before I wrap my arms around him. His body relaxes as he pulls me closer.

Tears trickle down my face as I realize Porter was right about more than one thing. I haven't lost everyone I love.

"I'm okay, Etta," he says.

I struggle to catch a breath as I lean back to look at him.

He's beaten and bruised. Reid knows his brother isn't here, but he isn't giving up. There's a strength inside Reid that has never wavered. Even when Penn took his last breath, he was just as brave. And for four years, that's what I've longed to find—courage that comes from deep within.

As I help Reid onto his feet, he doesn't try to shove me away this time. "So this is it," he murmurs, glancing around the cavern. "Where do we go now?"

I bite my lip, unsure if I should admit that I don't exactly know. The map in my memories ends at the entrance in this cave, and a tremor runs down my spine as I recall how Porter ordered me not to enter the Maze this way.

Greer and the others reside in the heart of the prison, but the outskirts are filled with traps and obstacles that were too danger-ous to dismantle. Stay away from there.

Lifting my chin, I point to a stairway chiseled into the cave wall, knowing our only option is to press on. "There."

Reid leans on me as we stumble through the soft sand.

When I put my foot on the first step, a loud *click* sounds throughout the cavern.

We don't have time to react before a rounded cage drops through the darkness over the top of us. The sand beneath our boots funnels away to reveal a steel plate. Each cage bar locks into a small hole around the perime-ter, trapping us like birds.

My knees crash into the metal plate as some unseen lever pulls us higher and higher. The air whooshes past us as we rush up, then stop so abruptly that I land on top of Reid before scrambling over to the edge.

I scream as the black water from the cave ripples far below us.

"No!" Reid shouts, pushing himself to his feet. The cage barely clears the top of his head, and there's hardly enough space for two. He wraps his hands around the bars and pulls.

"Stop," I yell as we swing from side-to-side. Whatever the top of this cage is attached to lets out a horrific groaning sound, and I'm terrified if it breaks, we'll plunge into the water still trapped inside. I feel all around us. No locks, no keys. Nothing.

Ahead is the top of the stairway, which leads to a pathway through more sea caves. This view feels like a mind game, the semblance of freedom but there's no way out.

Reid collapses beside me, his breathing labored and rough. He's trembling badly enough that the cage is shaking. "Why didn't Porter warn you about this?"

"He tried," I say, ashamed to admit it. "He made me promise that we wouldn't come this way. I knew there were traps left over from when it was a prison, but I figured we had to risk it to find Greer in time." Clutching my head, I want to tell Reid something reassuring. Promise that I'll find some way to get us out of here, but I can't bring myself to lie to him. "I'm sorry . . . I'm so sorry," I say over and over again.

"Etta, stop," Reid says, sounding so much like Penn that it makes me cry harder.

"Even if we break out of this cage, who knows what's waiting for us out there?" I point at the sea caves. "I was stubborn and stupid, and I never should've brought us here!"

"We'll get through this," he says.

I roughly wipe a tear away. "You're just like Penn, do you know that? Selfless and brave—everything I always wanted to be. He was the best person I've ever known, and I loved him." Shivering, I tuck my head toward my chest as my throat closes, and I can't bring myself to tell Reid that I feel the same way about him. I whisper, "I would've done anything to save your brother."

After a few seconds, Reid draws closer and wraps his arm around me. But he's so weak that his skin feels barely warmer than mine. "I know," he whispers back.

My heart aches at his words. It's not forgiveness, but it's a start. I lean my head on his shoulder and squeeze my eyes shut as tears roll down my cheeks. But the longer we sit in silence, my fear of the Maze dissolves into fury. Because if we don't get out of here, it isn't just Reid I've failed, but Penn too.

I push away from Reid and hit the bars with my fist

over and over again, refusing to believe we made it this close to Greer only to end up here.

"That's not going to do much of anything," says a low voice, the words echoing throughout the cavern. "Never once has someone broken out of that cage."

Reid moves slightly in front of me as a shadow appears at the top of the stairs.

"It's been quite a while since anyone has washed up on this shore. Care to tell me what happened to bring you here?" In our silence, he holds up something that looks like a key. "If you ever want out of there, I'll need an answer. I know full well nobody comes here by accident. What'd you do to get thrown into Minder training, hmm?" He steps closer, but his face is still hidden by the darkness. "Most days, an enemy of those soldiers is a friend of mine, but sharing an enemy doesn't make us allies now, does it?"

I feel my mouth drop open. His voice is deeper, but if my memory serves me right—and I have no doubt it does—it's a Shadow who went missing long ago, presumed dead, the same as me.

Beau.

"Beau!" I scramble to my feet and clutch the bars. "Beau, is that you?"

He angles his head. "Has the tide dragged you in here before? That sea's a tricky beast."

"It's Etta, I mean Jules! Julietta Lark!"

Reid jumps up to stand beside me. "Wait . . . that's Beau? The Shadow who went missing?"

"Julietta Lark died four years ago," Beau says, his words razor-sharp.

I loop my tangled hair into a knot out of my face. "It's me. I swear it."

As Beau steps into the beam of light, I finally get a good look at him. He focuses on my tattoos before switching to my face. He looks older, a scar across his left cheek he didn't have four years ago. It's jagged and rough across his kind face, though I'd recognize him anywhere. I'm about to rattle off the dozens of memories we made together when he throws his head back and puts his hands on his knees.

"Julietta Lark, it is you!" he cries and jams the key into a lock hidden in the cave wall.

I let out a cry of joy as the cage begins traveling down, much slower than the trip up. The steel plate clicks into a base at the bottom of the stairs and slowly, the bars rise into the darkness.

With a roar of laughter, Beau opens his arms, and I step out of the cage to hug him tightly.

"How'd you know we were here?" I ask.

"The cage is connected to a bell in the only part of the Maze we use nowadays. It rings like crazy whenever we catch someone." Beau draws back and studies my face. "You grew up, Jules."

I grin, sure I'm a sight with the cut on my cheek and dripping wet with seaweed in my hair. "And your dimples went away."

Half his mouth dips into a smile. "Well, I left them in Kripen. Spent nearly two years there."

I feel sick at the thought. Craewick isn't exactly a safe haven, but I can't imagine living as a prisoner of the Minders. I felt enough like one in Craewick, but I'm sure the fray would be lavish in comparison to Kripen.

"I'm so sorry, Beau," I tell him.

"You're not the one who locked me up."

"But I betrayed the one who would've gotten you back," I say quietly.

"You were a kid who made a choice to save your mother. That, Jules, anyone can understand. But what are you doing here? And who's this?" He eyes Reid's wrist. "Tattoos don't usually drip off, my friend, so I've already got a good feeling about you."

To have Beau forgive me means more than I could ever say. I introduce the two then ask, "Greer . . . is he here?"

"'Course he's here. But how'd *you* find us?"

Grinning, I clutch Beau's arm. Greer's so close! I quickly explain getting the map from Porter.

Beau nods. "Greer told me about the connection, but Madame told him you were dead. If we'd known you were alive, we would've come for—"

"It's best you didn't know, especially since the Maze has kept you safe." I glance up the steps, yearning to see my father. "Take me to him, Beau."

We follow Beau to the stone walkway through the sea caves. They're as pretty as coral reefs, twisting and curving above us in lovely designs.

"Step only on the darker rocks," he says, jumping onto a black boulder while carefully avoiding the colorful ones in between.

"Why?" I ask.

"Because anyone who doesn't winds up back in the sea." He jams his heel into a white rock and it flips on its side, revealing a hole big enough for someone to slip into the waves crashing just beneath it. "Stay close. The Maze is full of surprises."

My face warms as I consider what could've happened to us if Beau hadn't shown up.

Most of the caves are open at the top, beams of sunlight splashing onto the crystal blue water below as we jump from boulder to boulder. There are a few waterfalls trickling down the smooth rock walls, and others are covered with fuchsia flowers. I pluck one off the wall before Beau slaps it out of my hands.

"Pretty, aren't they?" he says. "They're also poisonous. One sniff will knock you out for hours. And it's not a peaceful sleep either, let me tell you. Whatever's in that pollen induces nightmares."

I steal a glance at Reid, who looks just as confused as I am. To think of my grandfather, with his serene gardens and deep love for the Aravid people, designing these kinds of mind games seems impossible to believe.

We veer down a tunnel with a roof of thick ivy and various fruits hanging off the vines. My stomach growls, loudly enough to echo off the rocky walls.

I put my hands up as Beau turns to face me. "I won't touch anything else. I've learned my lesson. Nothing in the Maze is what it seems."

"Well, you're exactly right, Jules. Nothing is quite what it seems." He grins before picking a berry to pop into his mouth. "If you're hungry, eat up."

The berries are delicious, both perfectly tart and sweet. "How'd you end up here, Beau? Did the Minders send you to the Maze?" I ask.

He glances over his shoulder. "In a way. After I woke up with a knife to my throat outside of Kripen, I spent months in a cage much like the one you found yourself in. That's when I vowed to break every lock the Minders put on me. And the first time they made me part of their target practice, I escaped into the sea, crashed into the side of the cave like your boy Reid here, and washed up on shore."

I stiffen, wondering how much Reid appreciates being called *my boy*, but he doesn't react.

"I couldn't recall my own name and had no idea where I'd been," Beau says. "I was as dazed as a Hollow, if you can imagine. Didn't remember a lick of the Shadows or Greer. It took him a while to convince me we weren't a couple of dead guys, but eventually my memories flooded back."

The air cools as we round a corner into a tunnel with dozens of black holes trailing down the center.

Beau presses up against the wall and cautions us to do the same. "Sand pits," he says, inching forward. "Nearly impossible to get out once you've set foot in one."

My heart races as we tiptoe between the sand pits and come to a set of stone steps leading down to a rusted metal door.

Beau strikes a match against the wall and lights a lantern hanging beside it. Then he lifts the door handle.

I let out a laugh as the wall beside us creaks open, an entrance to a stone passageway. It's so narrow I can't raise my arms, and Reid has to hunch over to avoid hitting his head. I have to order myself not to panic, especially when we're forced to turn sideways and squeeze between two boulders to get to the next tunnel.

This one is larger, but I wrinkle my nose at the stench of mold and dead fish as we up our pace. Even with Beau's lantern, it's so dark I can hardly see the iron doors built into the rocky walls.

Beau taps one as we pass. "Reinforced steel cells. Soundproof, impenetrable. Porter sure knew what he was doing when he designed this place. Between all the trapdoors and the twisting pathways, getting back to the surface is nearly impossible. That is, if the prisoner was unlucky enough to get out of his cell, of course."

"The Maze is underground?" Reid asks.

"Prisoners escaped from here?" I ask at the same time.

"Above, actually," says Beau to Reid, then looks at me. "Escaped? No. They were set loose. Most would spend a few weeks in those pitch-black boxes, only to think they'd been given freedom when the guards opened their doors. It didn't take long to realize there are much more frightening things than darkness down here."

A shiver runs down my spine. Porter designed the Maze to snatch whatever sanity his prisoners had left. How would it feel to be trapped inside this terrible game?

We pass through another musty tunnel of prison cells and up two more flights of steep stairs before I understand what Beau means about the Maze being above ground. There's a shaft to our right and another to our left but ahead is a huge open archway with a patch of blue sky and wispy clouds.

I peer over the edge. It's a long fall to the sea, down a jagged bluff. The waves crash against a cluster of boulders at the bottom.

"These heights dissuaded a lot of escapees from risking the jump to get out of here," says Beau. "But if given the choice, I'd rather have two broken legs and a shot at freedom, thank you very much."

I glance over the edge once more before Reid pulls me back.

"Watch your step," Beau says, pointing out a tiny wire running across the width of the tunnel. "I know this place better than most everyone here, but Porter was quite clever in their designs. These traps are nearly impossible to see and scattered all throughout the Maze. I still trip from time to time."

Reid and I both step over the wire before there's a

groaning sound from behind us. When I glance back, the walls have *moved*. Actually shifted around to where the hallway behind us is different than the one we just walked through.

"There are plates beneath our feet that sense movement through these channels. Once someone has passed through, the Maze changes. You can never go the same way twice," Beau says.

"It's almost poetic if it weren't so terrifying," I say flatly.

Beau laughs once. "Agreed."

Up ahead is a small pond filled with fish that glow and a giant waterfall rushing into it. There's so much water that it looks as if we're viewing a river at the wrong angle. As Beau wades into the pond, Reid and I exchange a look before we follow after him.

Schools of fish dart in between us, all swimming in unison as if they're one. They knock into our legs before rushing away.

"Don't make any sudden movements," Beau says. "They only attack when they feel threatened."

Reid tenses beside me, and his hand slips into mine after I almost lose my footing on the mossy stones under the water.

Beau disappears behind the waterfall, and I suck in a breath before I close my eyes and follow after him. The water soaks me to the bone. When I open my eyes on the other side, there's nothing but darkness. The waterfall roars behind us as I blink a few times before my eyes adjust.

We're standing on the thin, rocky ledge of another giant cavern, this one bigger than any of the ones before. But between us and the way out—a tiny beam of light which looks like a doorway on the opposite side of the cave—is a dark abyss.

"No!" I scream, reaching out as Beau walks right off the ledge.

He turns around, looking as if he's hovering in midair, before he taps his foot on something hard. "No need to be frightened. This here is the safest part of the Maze."

Reid and I draw closer, and I recoil as I look down, seeing nothing but darkness. I timidly take a step forward and see it's a bridge made of glass. So crystal clear that you'd never know crossing this abyss was possible unless you tried.

My heart is still pounding when I catch up with Beau and punch his shoulder. "Warn us next time!"

He gives me a sheepish grin and pats my cheek like he used to when I was a child. "Now there's the Jules I know."

I can't help but smile as I bat his hand away.

The doorway on the other side leads to a staircase that twists and curves, making it appear endless. I look up then down, but it's impossible to see where it begins or ends. It's also rotting away. Many steps and most of the rails are missing.

"These stairs look as fragile as a spider's web but they're stronger than any steel. Another one of your grandfather's inventions," Beau says.

The stairs are so steep that we have to practically climb to the top. I'm sweating and out of breath as we come to a landing and spill out of the last tunnel.

We're back in the open air, the sun shining brightly upon a wall of smooth, white marble as tall as the eye can see. Built into it is what looks like the remains of a castle, with huge turrets and chiseled archways.

I spin once to take it all in as we pass through a set of tall wooden doors, which leads into the main hall. The glass in the windows is gone, the breeze flooding in through the narrow frames warm and comfortable. A sprawling marble staircase leads up to a second-floor balcony overlooking the entire hall.

"This home has been in Porter's fam—your family—for generations." Beau jams his hands into his pockets, rocking back on his heels. "It's a bit different than you expected, eh?"

I can't find the words to answer. After Porter's gardens, it's the most beautiful place I've ever seen.

There are bushels of violets growing *everywhere*. They trail up the smooth stone walls, crisscross over the vaulted ceiling, and curl in delicate waves around the ornate banisters.

I look for Greer but don't see him among the gardeners

clipping violets. Others hold large woven baskets on their hips, gathering the flowers as soon as they're harvested. Most of them appear frail, their hands shaking like the addicts in the asylum, but one thing's very different. They're attentive, alert, and their faces warm with color.

"You're making Porter's compound?" I ask Beau.

Nodding, he grins. "Most of these folks were like me—victims of some kind of Minder experimentation. Some were even in a coma." Beau plucks a violet off a trellis and tucks it behind my ear. "It wasn't until I drank this compound that I remembered anything of who I was or where I'd been. I'd never wish the memories I spent as a captive upon my worst enemy." He touches his scar, then motions around us. "But the way I see it now, I wouldn't care much about helping these minds heal unless I'd gone through the process myself."

I smile, imagining my mother opening her eyes for the first time in years, but I feel a kind of sadness too. There are so many violets here, enough for everyone in the asylum and then some. How many could be saved if Madame didn't stand in our way?

Walking up the stairs to the balcony, I see him, clipping violets off stems trailing over the ledge. I catch my breath when my father's gaze meets mine. His dark hair is now speckled with gray, and there are a few more wrinkles around his blue eyes, but even from here I see the flecks of gold spread throughout them.

"Julietta?" His voice breaks halfway through, making my name sound as if he's addressing two people, as he walks toward me. "How can this be?"

Leaving Reid and Beau, I draw closer.

My lips beg to move, to pour out four years of apologies bottled up inside me. Conversations I'd whispered night after night because I believed my father was dead and I'd lost the chance to ask for his forgiveness. A tear slips down my cheek as he touches my face.

"It's me," I whisper.

He wraps his arms around me. Emotions as powerful as the day I betrayed him wash over my body. I break down as he draws me closer, crying as I lean my head on his chest.

"I . . . I never meant—" I say.

"Don't apologize for trying to save your mother's life. There's nothing more you could've done."

"But she's alive!" I say, pulling back to see his face when he learns the truth. "Mother is in a coma, but she's moving. Porter says the compound can bring her back to us."

The color seeps into Greer's tearstained face, a growing smile upon his lips, as he glances at the flowers around us. But violets aren't the only thing that can save her now.

As quickly as I can, I tell him about pledging to Bray and meeting with Porter. There is so much I wish to share with him, years of life that we've been forced to spend apart, but tomorrow is Auction Day.

"Madame is planning to take over the Realms. If we don't stop her, she'll destroy all of this," I say, motioning around us. "Bray thinks Porter is manipulating me to protect Madame, so the Shadows won't fight alongside the Woodland army. Porter, Felix, and their soldiers are trying to cripple Madame in Craewick before she has time to gather all her Minders, but they're only a distraction. They don't have the numbers to defeat her. I always thought she was indestructible, but you can show her otherwise."

Even in the midst of these odds, hope surges inside me.

The day I received the auction notice, I was broken and fragile. Alone. But standing here with Greer, I feel a strength more powerful than I've ever owned take hold of me. But it runs far deeper than me. Its roots are in my mother and Ryder, in Reid, Porter, Felix, Beau, and my father. And I want the people of the Realms to finally be given the chance to find this kind of strength too.

Greer looks past me at the others safe and protected in the Maze, his eyes hardening before he touches my face. "You've changed, Jules, in more ways than one."

"My variation?" I ask quietly, and he nods. "Something happened to me on the day I betrayed you. I went to Blare to try to protect Mother . . . Penn followed me there. The Minders swarmed us, and Penn," I take in a breath, "died in my arms. After that I was unreadable."

His hand tenses on my cheek. "Was there a flash of light when Penn died?"

My knees buckle. "Yes. Why?"

Greer pauses. "When I see a person, I sense their energy as a single unit, which I'm able to gather and shift to another. When the Gift passes through me, it looks like a bright light, but I don't keep it long enough that it becomes a part of me. Ever since you were little, your Gift was stronger than most, and I always suspected you might've inherited part of my variation. But yours works through touch."

"Are you saying I took Penn's Gift?" I ask, and he nods slowly. Wide-eyed, I glance at Reid, remembering he said he felt Penn's closeness in some way. Was it because of me?

"Penn could duplicate memories, so it's only logical that your energy is even greater than before. This unreadability," Greer gently touches my forehead, "is your thoughts moving too rapidly for even a Sifter to latch onto. Protecting your mind is the combination of yours and Penn's Gifts working together, two variations that formed something new."

I lean against the balcony to keep myself upright. How is it, even in death, Penn is still watching out for me? "I think I can use his variation too," I tell Greer, remembering how I accidentally gave Reid the memory of Penn's death. "I can share memories without losing the original."

"A powerful Gift," he murmurs.

As I look up at him, his lips aren't smiling but his eyes

are. I've always loved Greer, but he's never been sweet like my mother or kind like Porter and Felix. He was the leader of the Shadows, our unfailing protector. Even after all these years, he's still embodying what Porter encouraged me to find, an emotion that still hasn't left my father's face—peace.

Tears sting my eyes as I think about all we're about to do, exposing Greer as an adversary worthy of defeating Madame.

My father pulls me closer, whispering near my ear, "Madame already set out to destroy every piece of me and failed. This time will be no different."

I wrap my arms around him.

"Oh, Jules, I love you," he says quietly.

Bit by bit, I feel myself becoming whole once again. "And I love you, Father."

CHAPTER

20

I t's Auction Day.

Greer, Reid, and I reach the fray of Craewick just after sunrise. Smoke burns my eyes as black clouds billow above us from the direction of the square—a sure sign Porter's attack is underway. But what kind of evil has Madame unleashed to retaliate?

We have three goals: to subdue the Minders before their link to Madame is broken, to save my mother, and for Greer to steal Madame's Gift. The Woodland army is tasked with the first. The closer we get to Craewick, I'm terrified for Porter and Felix. Will Madame fight alongside her Minders? Or has she gone into hiding, ensuring her safety while manipulating her puppet soldiers? They'll do anything, kill anyone at her command. But where is she giving those orders from?

"Within eyesight," Greer told us before we left the Maze last night. "Her connection will be strongest if she can see what her Minders are doing."

"You think she'll be out in the open?" I asked.

"Well-guarded but yes. She won't leave the fate of her city to chance."

A terrible thought had hit me. "The asylum is the highest point of Craewick. It overlooks the entire square."

Greer met my eyes. "If your mother is still there, I'll find a way to draw Madame away before I take her Gift."

"*We'll* find a way," I told him.

"No, Jules, you'll stay here with Beau. He'll need help transporting the compound to Craewick after this battle is over." His face hardened as I opened my mouth to argue. "I lost you once. Don't make me go through that again."

"Don't make me either! This is just as much my fight as it is yours," I said, but Greer's expression didn't change. "I still have Porter's map. If you try to leave me here, I'll find my own way to Craewick. If something happens to you, Father—" My voice broke. "My place is beside you."

It was the first time I'd ever raised my voice to him. I braced myself for him to lock me up in one of the Maze's prison cells to keep me far away from Craewick, but his eyes softened as he touched my face.

"You've grown up, Jules. You look just like your mother, especially in that cloak."

I placed my hand on top of his. "So I've been told."

Brushing the memories away, I follow close behind Greer as we pass through the fray of Craewick. It's nearly deserted, save for a few elderly roaming about. Greer tells them to lock themselves in their homes. I'm hoping the reason my neighbors aren't here is because they've sought shelter deep in the woods.

When I think of Madame's hatred of the Ungifted, I have a terrible feeling that isn't the case. She's brainwashed countless Gifted soldiers. Manipulating the Ungifted would be almost too easy. What kind of twisted use could she come up with for them? And if we don't stop Madame today, it's not just those in the Realms who'll suffer but the Ungifted Tribes too.

I glance over at Reid. Beau gave him more of the compound, but between Bray's beating, hiking through Kripen, and crashing into the side of that cave, he's still not his old self. But his eyes are clear and alert. He's ready for this fight. I see it in the tenseness of his arms holding his bow, in the fearlessness I've sensed since the moment we met.

Closer to the square, the clash of metal and the screams are deafening. I don't see any Minders, but masses of people pack the alleys surrounding the square. Most are Hollows, bloody and pale as they flee from their once well-guarded homes. Reid stays close behind me as I fight to keep up with Greer, pushing against them.

The shops around us are all in flames. Thick smoke swirls out of shattered windows and fallen roofs. My lungs burn as I struggle to catch a breath, the air dark with soot and ash. Embers singe our clothes as we press against an alley wall.

I look out over the square at hordes of battling soldiers. For every Woodland Minder, their arms banded in purple, there are dozens wearing Stone Realm black or Desert Realm red. No blue for the Coastal Realm. I frantically search every face for Ryder's. Did something happen to her on the way, or has Sorien refused to help?

My father clutches my cloak and pulls me into his arms. "Whatever happens to me, get your mother out of Craewick," he says.

I nod against his chest, not sure how I'll ever be able to leave him. But I know my mother needs me more than Greer does.

He moves to the front of the alley, peering around the corner with his hand up to give us a signal to move.

Reid's already staring at me when I meet his gaze. "You blame yourself for what happened with my brother, but I want you to know that I don't. He loved you, Etta, and that never changed, right up until the moment he died."

A tear slips down my cheek as I smile at him. My head fills with warmth as sparks of his memory, the one

I accidentally stole outside the Maze, flutter across my mind. I still have this memory, but his feelings were powerful enough to create another.

I might not have the chance to tell her Penn's death wasn't her fault. That memory showed me she loved him as much as he loved her, and I understand why.

These past five days, I've seen a girl who owns the kind of strength that can never be bought. And if I never get to say it, I hope she knows I wish I did.

"This," Reid points out of the alley, "is a fight that'll honor Penn's memory. And there's nowhere I'd rather be than fighting beside you and your father."

Taking his hand, I slip Penn's bracelet off my wrist and slide it onto his. I'm terrified Reid is saying goodbye but in the midst of this, threads of hope appear. Hope for Craewick, hope for us, hope that all the bad that's happened the past four years has somehow led to this moment—a chance for something better once the worst is over.

Reid closes his hand around mine and draws it close to his heart.

"Now!" Greer yells.

Bolting out of the alley, we veer toward the asylum.

Steel scrapes against steel, creating a sharp hiss that makes me want to cover my ears. But swords aren't the only weapons. I leap over dozens of convulsing bodies on the ground, their muscles in spasms from their minds being read too quickly.

Someone throws a brick at the treasury.

I duck as the windows shatter, spraying glass onto the street.

Dozens of Collectors rush out. Gone are their smug expressions, their lavish clothes now wrinkled and bloody. One is sprawled out on the treasury steps, her limbs sticking out at odd angles. Blood flows from her nose. Her pupils are deathly white.

"Jules!" calls Greer, but I've lost sight of him and Reid in the swarm of Minders.

An arrow whizzes past, just missing my head. I stoop low as the archer—a Minder as young as Ryder—reloads. Swiping a thick shard of glass off the ground, I throw it at his thigh.

As he falls, I whip around, slamming into another Minder. I struggle against her as she clutches my arms. Blood blooms like a flower on her white shirt. Her cloudy eyes roll back into her head. We crash to the ground, the metals on her uniform rattling as she pins me on the blood-soaked street.

Gritting my teeth, I try to heave her off when I catch sight of her tattoo.

Ungifted and dressed like a commander?

I cry out when I see the dead man beside me, reaching out toward his fallen son. Both lived in the fray. His hands are calloused and rough, still covered in dirt like they always were when he returned from the fields.

They were farmers and yet here they are, dressed like soldiers.

I let out a scream. I can almost hear Madame threatening the Ungifted, ordering them from the safety of the fray to the square. Once they're in a Stone Realm uniform, how can the Woodland Minders tell the difference between an innocent or a foe? Fury gives me the strength to heave this poor woman off me, then Greer pulls me to my feet.

I call out Reid's name as I look at the alleys winding around the square, packed with soldiers. Their faces are white with terror, many covered in blood. Panic rises up inside me. I see flashes of black and red, of Stone and Desert soldiers slicing through the Woodland army. They're like bees rushing out from a hive, more and more billowing into the square as if their numbers are endless.

And if Greer dies here, there'll be no one left to stop Madame.

I'm jerked off my feet when a Craewick Minder tries to wrench me away from Greer, but Father doesn't let me go until the Minder collapses.

All around us, soldiers clutch their chests or their heads, falling to the ground before they get close to us.

Greer's breathing hard, sweat trickling down his face, but I've never seen him look more alive. He's stealing memories so quickly these Minders don't stand a chance.

I swing my bow off my back as a commander with bright gold flecks in her eyes barrels toward him.

She plunges her knife into Greer's arm.

In a flash, Greer pulls it out, but she jumps back before he can stab her.

I nock my last arrow and fire at her leg.

When the Sifter falls, Greer cracks his elbow down on her temple and knocks her out.

But there are still too many and we're only two.

I spy Reid near the auction stage, fighting through a group of Minders to get to us. I scream as a soldier behind him lifts her sword. But before she can slam it across Reid's skull, the tip of an arrow pokes out from her heart.

It isn't until the Minder drops that I see who saved him.

Bray.

With his army of Shadows behind him.

CHAPTER
21

As Minders come between us, Bray takes them out one-by-one.

A woman with a bloodied knife crumbles to the ground as she charges him.

Pulling a knife from his boot, Bray slits a Minder's kneecaps before knocking a sword from the soldier's hands and driving it into his chest.

The area around his eyes is fiery red from the blinding powder and he's bloody from this battle, but there's a difference about Bray from when we last saw him in the Mines. Something familiar I recognize from a childhood spent together. There's a crack in his hardness, a flicker of what I always admired about him—his loyalty to Greer, Cade, and the Shadows.

Reid rushes up beside me.

I clutch his arm, searching for any sign that he's injured but find none. His eyes widen on my stained tunic before I tell him the blood isn't mine.

Bray meets Reid's stare, then mine. "For Cade, Joss, and Penn," he shouts.

"For our family," Reid yells back.

"For our family," I repeat, looking around us. "Some of the Ungifted are dressed like commanders. Don't kill them!"

With a nod, Bray glances at Reid. "Get her out of here."

Reid wraps his arm around me, pulling me toward the outskirts of the square as more Shadows rush in.

"Greer," I scream. "We can't leave without Greer!"

"He'll find us," Reid says, tightening his grip.

Some of the Shadows are dragging the Hollows out of the alleys and knocking out the Ungifted dressed like Minders. The others are fighting with such strength that the soldiers are forced to retreat. It's an awesome sight to see how confused these Minders are, thinking they'd won only to be blindsided by an army they didn't know existed.

The troops are quickly realigning when I spot Greer approaching Bray. I let out a cry of relief when I see he isn't hurt.

There's proudness in Greer's eyes as he looks at Bray, a respect deeper than a mentor and protégé but that of a father and a son. He puts his hand on Bray's shoulder, drawing him closer before Bray is swallowed up by the fight.

Minutes later, Greer, Reid, and I push against the people scurrying in and out of the asylum.

The first floor is mayhem. Not a nurse in sight and no one keeping order. Soldiers swarm the patients like flies, ripping memories from their minds.

I watch a boy strangling a woman until Greer knocks him out. Still, her chest heaves up from the bed. Her eyes bulge as a terrifying laugh flies out of her throat.

Once up the stairs, we're forced to slow down because of the bodies on the floor. It's disgusting to see these patients crumpled like trash, abandoned by the nurses who pledged to protect them. I want to clean their bloodied lips and put them back in their beds, but most are already dead. Like poor Baldwin. His white, lifeless eyes are wide open, a look of anguish on his pale face.

A shadow moves behind the curtain near my mother's bed.

Greer swipes the knife off his belt and nods at me.

I grasp the thin fabric and rip the curtain open.

Her back toward us, Madame stares out the window overlooking her burning city. The auction stage far below is up in flames. An explosion rocks the asylum's foundation, but she doesn't flinch.

What surprises me more than seeing Madame is that

my mother is still in her bed. She looks unharmed, her face molded in the same expressionless position it's held for four years. But today, her condition comforts me. She knows nothing of the turmoil around her. Not yet, anyway.

I want to run to her, but Reid puts his arm in front of me as Greer approaches Madame.

"I've been waiting for you," Madame says in a cool, soft tone. She still has her back to us, but I have a feeling if we shot an arrow, she'd be quick enough to catch it. "Father, mother, and daughter, all reunited in this very room. How poetic."

My entire body tenses. How did Madame discover that Greer is my father? The only people who knew the truth were far away from Craewick the whole time I've been gone, except for . . . I glance at my mother.

"Let Gwen go," Greer says in a voice lower than I've ever heard from him.

"And why would I do that?" Madame slowly turns, the flecks in her eyes ablaze. Her head tips to one side as her gaze meets mine.

I clench my jaw at the slight raise of her eyebrows, at how she makes me feel as if she's reading my every thought.

Madame angles toward Greer. "There's more strength in my army than the Woodland soldiers and the Shadows combined. I own a power greater than you'll ever know."

She has a knife at my mother's throat before we have time to react. "But your Gwendolyn is the only thing I ever needed to defeat you."

Greer steps forward, but when the knife draws a drop of blood on my mother's neck, he stops.

"No, no. Not so close," says Madame lightly. "I know all your secrets, Greer, but shall I tell you how I discovered them? I would've destroyed Gwendolyn's mind long ago, but she's proven to be rather useful to me."

His hands lock into fists by his sides.

Madame traces my mother's face with the tip of the blade. "For four years, her memories have been fractured, spliced together in ways that made it impossible to distinguish fact from fiction. But when she began healing and all those tiny veins of memory were reconnected, the strength of her mind surprised me. I read her to find more information about Porter, but seeing you," she points to my father, a wicked grin on her face, "was a lovely surprise. Deep, deep, deep within Gwendolyn's mind, there were tiny fragments of memory that revealed your greatest secrets—not only are you Julietta's father but I know you own a variation unlike any other." She twists her head in my direction. "I believed Greer was dead. You should've let your father stay buried in that Maze, Julietta, because losing everyone you love all in one day . . ." She clicks her tongue. "What a tragedy it will be."

I force myself to hold to the truth. Madame may have

fewer, tinier cracks than most but we just need to find one big enough that we can slip through.

"And who might you be?" she says with a glance at Reid. "Oh, another Sifter . . ." She spits out a laugh at me. "Who knew you had friends other than that runt of an orphan?"

Reid holds me back when I lunge at her.

"I will make myself very clear. If you wish your Gwendolyn to live, you will do exactly as I say," says Madame to Greer, mock sorrow on her face. "Because if you don't, your precious daughter will watch her mother die before suffering the same fate."

My fingers twitch, aching to clasp her throat.

"If you can really transfer Gifts, then what I want is unreadability," Madame seethes, pointing at me with the tip of her knife. "Take her Gift and give it to me."

"Never," says Greer.

"Oh, but the hour is young." She slices the knife across my mother's forearm.

I scream. The hardest thing isn't seeing the river of blood on her thin gown, or the way my father jerks forward so I have to pull him back. It's how my mother reacts. She trembles, her expression briefly one of anguish.

"If that isn't stitched up in minutes, she'll bleed out long before she'll wake from her coma. Tick, tock, Greer," Madame says. "Tick, tock."

Greer clutches my neck and whispers, "I'm sorry, Jules. Trust me."

I've never felt anything but trust for him. But as pain explodes at the base of my skull, I jerk out of his grasp. My sight dissolves into white flecks, my temples pulse in sharp beats. I stumble before my legs collapse.

Reid wraps his arms around me and lowers me down.

Curling into myself, I will this pressure to dissolve, frantically searching for answers. How was Greer able to take my Gift with my unreadability? This fire lit deep within terrifies me, proving that nothing's impossible.

As Madame watches me withering on the floor, a ghost of a smile haunts her lips. "Give it to me. Now."

"Open your mind," Greer says. "It won't work unless you put your guard down."

She presses the knife against my mother's throat. "Do not test me."

"Open your mind," he repeats through gritted teeth as he steps toward her, "and I will give you what you want."

As my Gift seeps into Madame, her eyes flash with light, glowing as brightly as the sun. Her body trembles as she cries out.

Greer collapses in front of her. The knife in his hand, now covered with blood, clatters on the tile beside me. He clutches his chest, some unseen wound opened the instant he shifted my energy into Madame.

She whips her head in my direction, her smile growing until she meets my eyes. Her face twists with rage before she screams, "You're still . . . you're still unreadable!"

Greer is too weak to fight back as she slams his head against the wall. "What did you do?" she shrieks.

Warmth drips down my neck. I touch the base of my skull and wince at the pain. My fingers are soaked with blood. I grind my teeth at the wave of nausea. Greer nicked me near a bundle of nerves, but why? I squeeze my eyes shut as Madame lunges toward me.

Reid steps between us.

"The energy around you . . . I can see it now." She gazes at Reid, a hunger in her expression that makes me shudder. "It's *glorious*." She clutches Greer's collar, whispering near his ear, "If you thought you could protect your daughter by giving me your Gift instead of hers, you've never been more wrong."

I tremble, now understanding why Greer cut me. He fooled Madame into opening her mind by making her believe he'd stolen my Gift. But all along, he'd been planning to sacrifice his.

She laughs long and hard as she throws Greer toward me. "You will live just long enough so I can see the look on your face when I kill them. Porter, Gwendolyn, Julietta. Every single one."

Reid grabs Madame by the neck and slams her to the ground.

Madame arches her back, throwing Reid off before he can stab her.

When she kicks his knee, Reid yells as he collapses, his leg at such an odd angle that I know it's broken.

Crawling toward my father, I pull him close as his energy dissolves, his skin cooling beneath my fingers. It's too similar to Penn's death that my memories play with me, weaving between this moment and the one when I lost my best friend.

"Father," I cry, and his eyelids flutter open.

"Let her take your Gift," he murmurs between ragged breaths. "Give her what she wants. Trust me. Your mother is coming back, Jules, she's right here with you." His arms go limp, the flecks in his eyes fading. "We'll always be together."

Something inside me quivers and breaks as Madame's bony hand clutches my shoulder. I recoil at her grin, but it's my mother who distracts her.

My mother shudders, her chest lifting high as she gasps for air.

"Mother!" I say, but her eyes are sealed shut, her body as still as it's been the past four years.

"Weak," Madame hisses.

As I look up at her, I see years of auctions and our cottage in Blare caught up in flames. I hear her giving orders to slit Cade's throat and kill Joss. If Madame wins, the Ungifted Tribes will be hunted and slaughtered. The other Realms attacked and subdued to quench her lust for power. But before she does any of this, Madame will murder my family one-by-one.

Laying my father gently on the ground, I rise to my feet and meet Madame's stare. "If you want my Gift, come and take it."

"Etta, no!" shouts Reid. His raises himself up on his elbows but collapses once he puts weight on his knee.

My challenge only widens Madame's smile as I pick up the knife, flexing my fingers around the hilt.

"That will not save you, little one. Nor will it save this boy you love," she says.

Darting around Madame, I lunge toward my mother. She's convulsing, slips of air passing between her pale lips. Slipping a vial of compound from my pocket, I empty it onto her bleeding wound. "Stay with me, Mother," I cry.

Outside of the asylum, the roar of battle grows even louder.

I look out the window. More Minders have joined in the fight . . . Minders wearing the color of the Coastal Realm. Hope rushes up inside me.

Madame clutches my throat and pins me against the wall. "You are full of so many secrets, Julietta. Let's see if your mind will finally open once you die."

Scorching hot blood courses through my head, flames licking my brain. My thoughts are jumbled as memories spark behind my eyelids.

Cade smiles, laughs a little. Joss puts her hand over her

heart. Penn looks at me as if I'm the most beautiful thing he's ever seen. I know forever and ever, I will love him. All of them.

As quickly as they appear, my friends fade away. First Cade, then Joss. Penn is the hardest to let go. I'm tempted to join them. To give up as Madame has always wanted. Instead I thrash and scream. She tried to use my past to destroy me, but it's the weapon I need to keep fighting. The love of those who gave up their lives for me.

My vision dims, a black cloud descending upon the queen of Craewick. But I don't want the last image I see to be of hurt and hatred. I close my eyes and think of my father, my mother, and Reid when the world explodes.

CHAPTER
22

I scrunch cool wet sand between my toes as the balmy air kisses my face.

The waves are soft and low as the seabirds fly just above our heads, their calls mixing with the sound of my mother's voice.

Softly singing, she swipes her brush across her canvas, painting a scene as beautiful as the one spread out before us.

Glancing up from my easel, I look over at my mother's. A hurried sketch has transformed into something extraordinary, the face of a man I've never seen before. His eyes are as blue as the sky, and his face doesn't need a smile to appear kind.

"Who is that?" I ask her.

She kisses the top of my head. "Someone who showed me what love truly is."

Blackness envelops me. I scream, but nothing comes

out. I'm trapped inside my body as this coma steals what's left of the light. A better thief than I ever was.

My father pulls me closer, whispering near my ear, "Madame already set out to destroy every piece of me and failed. This time will be no different."

I wrap my arms around him.

"Oh, Jules, I love you," he says quietly.

Bit by bit, I feel myself becoming whole once again. "And I love you, Father."

A spark comes from my fingertips. Warmth travels up my arms and floods my chest. My heart beats in my ears, its rhythm drawing me *back, back, back*. There's a hand in mine. With all the strength I find, I tap my finger three times.

My baby girl. It's a slight whisper, so faint I know it's only my mind telling me what I wish to hear. *I love you too.*

Through the slits of my eyes, I see my mother smiling down at me.

Her cheeks are stained with tears, and her blonde hair is longer than it's ever been. The side of her mouth droops to the left. One eye is cloudy, and she's frail, her collarbone jutting out from beneath her billowy top, but I've never seen her look more beautiful in my entire life.

I hug her tightly, not sure I'll ever be able to let go.

As she strokes my hair, I soak up the warmth of her skin on mine. I feel the strong beat of her heart and let myself cry. No longer fighting the emotions I was too afraid would shatter me. I let go of the regret, sadness, longing, and fear that this moment would never come.

It's a while before I draw back, only to look at her face, to watch her speak as if she hasn't been in a coma the past four years.

"You're awake!" I cry.

"I was trying so hard to come back to you, my sweet," she says, the love I hear in her voice telling me she would've spent a hundred more years fighting her coma. "I heard you while I slept and felt your hand in mine. You gave me the strength to keep fighting."

"But it was all my fault, Mother," I whisper.

"No, darling girl, you *saved* me. This coma protected me. It kept Madame from reading my mind and gaining information she would've used against my father. If he'd been forced to submit to her four years ago, the Realms wouldn't have been given the chance for rebirth." She takes my face in her hands. "Your father and I always hoped that you'd grow up in a world full of light, but what a privilege and an honor to be a part of what destroyed the darkness. I'm so proud of you, Julietta."

As she pulls me close, I see an empty bed over her shoulder, where I imagine my father should be.

I've never felt quite like this. Such happiness with my mother coming back to me as I try to comprehend my father never will. I finally understand what Reid meant about the energy which joined him to Penn. A connection now severed that hurts in a place so deep it's hard to catch a breath.

My mother follows my gaze. "His heart . . . without the energy of his Gift, it gave out—" A sob catches in her throat. "Your father would do it all over again to save you."

"But you never had the chance to say goodbye," I say.

"Oh, but I did, my love." She smiles through her tears as she takes my hands in hers. "Before he died, he gave me memories more precious than I've ever known. Times of you growing up with the Shadows, the joy he felt getting to know his daughter. They're all with me now." She touches her heart. "You both gave me the power to break free of the coma."

I clutch her tighter, reminded of when she shuddered before she woke, of how my father spoke of her coming back before he died. It wasn't his mind slipping but connecting with hers.

"She's coming back, Jules, she's right here. We'll always be together."

"My heart is heavy," my mother says, "but the love I have for him will never disappear, not when it was built on something more than just the two of us. Even through the pain of believing he'd lost us both long ago, your father never stopped trusting there was good in the world worth fighting for. And if he can trust in that," she kisses the top of my head, "we can too. The joy of knowing him will help us through the sorrow of saying goodbye."

Through my memories, I see my father as I've always known him. Housing a strength that came from a place Madame could never find or take away. He watches us from beside the window of my mother's asylum room. He's smiling, eyes glistening, and I begin to believe my mother's words. That in the midst of heartache, his hope for the future only grew deeper roots.

"And you, Julietta, are a legacy that we couldn't be more proud of," my mother whispers.

I hug my mother once again, overcome as I witness the strength my parents found together and apart as they fought their own battles and came out victorious.

My heart swells when I hear my grandfather's voice outside the curtain.

"Oh, my girls, my lovely girls!" he says, kissing my brow and then my mother's.

There isn't a hint of hatred on my mother's face, and I know of the many things that happened while I slept, their reunion will be one I wish to hear about.

"You gave us quite a scare, Julietta. How are you feeling?" he asks.

"Better now that you're here too," I say. "You did it, Grandfather. You saved Craewick."

He touches my cheek, his face lighting up at his new title. "I'm not sure I had as much to do with it as you, child. Thanks to you and your father, Madame is downstairs under lock and key, the Gifts inside her destroyed along with much of her mind."

Sighing with relief, I touch my throbbing head. "There was an explosion and a flash of light before I blacked out. What happened between us?"

"She tried and failed to take your Gift." My grandfather pauses, his eyes shifting back and forth. "It's a hunch, but I believe your unreadability reflected Madame's own energy back onto herself, like sunlight on a mirror. Though repelling such a large amount of energy caused you to lose consciousness, your mind appears to be unaffected. You're even stronger than I imagined."

"So that's why Father transferred his Gift to her," I mummer. "He knew she'd come after my unreadability."

"And destroy herself in the process. Madame failed to realize the higher she raised herself up, the harder her fall would be." He takes my hand and then my mother's. "There's nothing more I wish than for Greer to be here, but I'm very thankful he lived to see the good he was able to do."

Clutching his hand, I sink back into the pillow as my mother rests her head on top of mine. Madame is no longer a threat, but what a high price we had to pay for her demise. Though as hard as it is to accept that Greer is gone, I feel a peace I can't quite explain. It isn't only his sacrifice which makes me proud to be his daughter, but like my mother said, the way he always lived for something greater than himself.

The curtain whips open, revealing a grinning Felix and an elated Ryder.

"I knew you'd wake up!" she cries, jumping onto the bed and pulling me close. "We did it, Etta. Can you believe we really did it?" She draws back. "You should've seen the fight. After you destroyed Madame, her Minders got this glazed look in their eyes right before they went after one another. They were punching and stealing memories off their own allies. It was total chaos." Ry grins at Felix. "We took them down after that, didn't we?"

"We did, my girl." Felix kisses my forehead. "You're incredibly brave, Julietta, just like your mother and this little one." He swings his arm around Ryder. "I'm told she marched into Craewick right alongside Sorien and his entire army."

"That sounds about right," I say, grinning at Ryder before I glance at the curtain. "And is Reid . . . ?"

"He's barely left this room for two days, my sweet. He should be back at any," my mother glances behind her and smiles as Reid appears, "moment."

I sit up.

His leg is splinted, there are stiches above his eye, and a deep bruise across his cheek. "Etta," he says softly.

My mother pats my hands and mouths, *We'll give you some time.* She swings her arm around Felix, who helps her into a chair with tiny wheels beside my bed. "How about something to eat, hmm?" she asks Ryder.

Ry holds her hand and walks beside her, while my grandfather follows close behind.

Unspoken words feel heavy between us, but I can't bring myself to speak to Reid. Gone is the rigid stance, the hard lines of his face. In the clear contentedness of his expression, he looks just like this brother as he takes the chair beside me.

"I thought I'd lost you," he says.

I let out a quiet laugh. "I'm not that easy to get rid of."

"Etta, I'm not joking. You were just lying there, not moving. Pale as could be. If you wouldn't have made it—"

When I put my hand on his, it's the energy I feel in his skin that tells me all I wish to know. That after all that's happened, he's willing to trust me again. "You were right about me," I whisper.

"Right about what?"

"About everything. I pushed you away and you kept coming back. You never gave up on me," I say. "And I promise that as long as I live, I'll honor your brother's memory."

"You already did." He strokes my cheek with his finger. "Most everyone in Craewick owes their life to Greer, Penn, and you. The three of you saved us all."

As my mother sleeps in the bed beside mine, Grandfather, Ryder, and Reid stay up with me all night. My grandfather pours out stories about his true loves—my grandmother Violet and my mother, her spunk and lively spirit that was bold enough to fight for a life with my father.

I drink up his words, spinning together my history with each tale. I look at my grandfather and then at Ryder, wondering how all these different threads of my life have somehow been beautifully braided together.

Reid catches my eye and grins.

And I know I'm finally home.

CHAPTER
23

A month has passed since we brought war to Craewick. A month since my mother woke from her coma and my father gave up his life for me. When my grandfather received a granddaughter on his doorstep, Madame was knocked off her throne, and the city of Craewick changed from gray to color.

The bloodstains have been scrubbed from the cobblestones, the remains of the auction stage chopped and stacked for firewood as we soak in the last days of autumn and prepare for the winter ahead.

It's been a long time since I've woken to screams, but tonight they're back. Not mine but Ryder's, coming through the thin wall we share between our bedrooms.

I light a candle and tiptoe into the hallway of the

orphanage, once Madame's mansion. It feels so much bigger without all the orphans scurrying about every which way. Mother tucked them in one-by-one hours ago.

Ryder's door creaks open as I let myself in. "Ry?"

She stirs but doesn't wake.

I sit on the edge of her bed, gently rubbing her shoulder.

She gasps, rousing out of sleep with a quickness that startles me. Her face is flushed and sweaty as she lets out long breath and rubs her eyes. "Etta," she whispers. "Did I wake you? I just . . . she was . . ." Ry glances around her room. "*She* was here."

Setting the candle on her bedside table, I ask, "Madame?"

"I'm not afraid during the day," Ry says quickly as I nod and give her my 'of course not' look, "but at night, everything changes. It's like I can feel her here."

"Plotting her revenge?" I guess. "She can't, Ry. She's not even strong enough to get out of her asylum bed."

She props her pillow up behind her, brushing a mess of curls away from her face. "What if my heart knows that but my head doesn't believe it?"

A question I've asked myself too. Some days I wake wondering if I'm back in the old Craewick. That the darkness of night has given Madame her power, given my mother her coma, and given my father back to the Maze.

"Move over," I tell her, and she gives me room to lean back on her pillow. "Remember what you told me the day we got Mother's auction notice? That when I planned to fight the Minders—"

"You wouldn't have to do it alone," she finishes.

"You knew way before me that some people are better together than apart," I say, nudging her softly. "And you know what's different about Craewick now? It isn't just Madame who lost her power, but the people of Craewick finally found theirs. She thought weakness was relying on anyone but herself, but in the end, it was the only way to defeat her. You showed me that, Ry. You're the bravest person I know."

She lets out a faint laugh. "I don't feel brave."

"Well, as someone very wise once told me, being brave doesn't mean you aren't afraid of anything. Just that the fear doesn't stop you from fighting for something you believe in."

"Did Grandfather say that?"

I grin. "Who else?"

It's been a few days since Ryder's adoption into our family became official, but the thing I'll remember most is when she pulled me aside at Grandfather's celebratory dinner and said, "You know I'm all for parties and presents, but you've already been my sister for as long as I can remember."

Ry smiles, wiggling her toes on top of the blanket. "Nah, you're the brave one, Etta. You're the one who saved everyone out there."

"Nah." I rest my head on top of hers. "I'm pretty sure it's the other way around."

On my way back to bed, I pass my mother sitting on the stone hearth of the fireplace, still glowing with embers. She looks up from my journal, the one I promised to give her after she woke, spread across her lap. Around her neck is the tiny key to its lock, dangling on a silver chain just like the one my grandfather gave to me. It's a sight that warms my heart, but tears sting my eyes as I imagine how my father should be beside her.

"Hello, my love," she says. "I peeked into Ryder's room, but it seems a talk with her sister is all she needed."

I meet her smile and sit, resting my head on her shoulder as she wraps her blanket around us. I glance at the journal entry she's been staring at, a charcoal sketch of my father. "I've missed him for four years, but this is a different kind of hurt," I say, touching the corner of the page. "I can't stop thinking about him."

"To be given hope only to have it taken away again . . . It's a different kind of sorrow," she says, tucking a wisp of hair behind my ear. "Hardly a minute goes by when I don't think of him, but in a way, isn't that a lovely thing, Julietta? To be so loved that you're always near one's thoughts? I see him every day through the memories we made together, and the ones he gifted me with of you. Your father gave me the greatest blessings I could ever ask for."

"I'm so proud of him," I say. "Even after he thought

he'd lost us, he forgave Grandfather. He took all the bad that happened between them and changed it into something so powerful that Madame couldn't defeat it."

She kisses the top of my head. "Learning to love again might not have been easy for him, but when we keep fighting to see the good in this world, our hearts will only grow stronger. Your father honored our memory, and now we get the chance to honor his."

⊶

The next afternoon, Reid and I linger at the stairs of the asylum. I take in the steep steps, noticing how this tall, narrow building doesn't seem frightening anymore. Not with bushels of violets spilling out of the urns beside the door, and a fresh coat of paint on the bricks.

"You sure you don't want me to come with you?" Reid asks for the umpteenth time today.

"I do want you with me," I say. "But I think I should see Madame alone."

"You don't have to see her today, Etta. You don't have to see her at all."

I ponder it for a moment, the nagging feeling I've tried to ignore for weeks flaring up inside me. My grandfather tells me I won't recognize Madame, but after my talk with Ryder, I want to see her, if only to be assured she's no longer capable of the evil she unleashed in this city.

"All the memories I have of her need an ending," I say.

Reid nods, understanding even if he doesn't feel the same way. "She isn't a threat anymore. Not now, not ever. You made sure of that."

"Well, I had pretty good partners."

"Is that so?"

I angle toward him. "Now that you mention it, *one* was just all right. Kind of demanding, a bit moody." I tell my lips to knock off the smiling, but they don't listen. Reid opens his mouth but I hold my hand up. "Oh, I'm not finished. Very stubborn, overprotective . . ."

He grins. "He feels the same way about you."

"Is that so?" I say, my smile fading as I stare up at the building. "I've built up all these images of Madame in my head, but the truth is she's locked up in her own asylum, isn't she?"

"She is. But besides that, you've always been stronger than you think. At least you know that now," he says, and I remember how he helped me believe that on our journey to Aravid. Back when I thought strength was something that once lost could never be found again.

"Maybe this strength has more to do with who's standing beside me," I say.

He smiles faintly. "I'll wait for you at Porter's. Felix found some old maps in Madame's desk that he wanted to show me. Thought I'd bring Ry along."

"She'll love that."

Ever since she met him, Ryder's been about all-things-Felix, an endless spring of questions concerning the Minders, their training methods, and battle techniques. *A little commander in the making,* Felix calls her.

For weeks, Reid and I have been plotting where the Ungifted Tribes could be. It won't be easy to find them, as for years they even managed to outsmart Madame. But we have a good idea who might have clues—the Hunters. They know every inch of the forest better than we ever will, and we're hoping a certain wolf boy and fox girl might be willing to work with us.

I long to meet Reid's mother and sister, but I can't pretend I'm not frightened by the idea. Because of me, they lost a son and a brother. Yet I yearn to thank the family of the boys who taught me life's truest joys can't be bought.

At the top of the steps, I turn to glance at Reid, reminded of what my grandfather said during our stroll through the woods yesterday.

"Reid looks so calm now. Peaceful, even."

"He's always looked like that, Grandfather," I say. The bruises have healed, and the cut above his eye is a small scar. Though he's limping, I don't see much of a difference from when I first met him. "He's a Sifter with the world spread out before him and doesn't want any of it. He's always known exactly who he is."

Pushing through the door, it's difficult to take in all the changes that've occurred in the asylum the past month. It was one of the few buildings that survived the battle, and it's been filled with patients ever since. Only this time, they're actually on the mend, far more being checked-out than checked-in.

A few days after my grandfather assumed control of Craewick, Beau arrived with barrels of the violet compound, along with those who lived in the Maze. Most spend their days here, their knowledge of the healing process invaluable. They're living proof of how well the compound works, giving hope to those who need it most.

Unlike my mother, whose mind had four years to heal before receiving the compound, most of these patients will be here for a while. Some need physical healing—mostly Gifted soldiers who were able to protect themselves from attacks of the mind. Many of the Ungifted are working on regaining their memories and coming out of comas. It'll be a long process, I know full-well, but nothing compares to hearing a loved one's voice again. The happiness far outweighs any past sorrow.

Clutching the pendant of my necklace, I stand outside Madame's room, where my mother once slept.

"Why should we show her mercy?" asks the Minder stationed here. "She would murder us all."

I smile sadly, reminded of what Greer once told Bray, and pull the curtain open. "Because there should be a difference between her and us."

Curled on her side, Madame looks small now, the opposite of the intimidating woman atop the auction block. Her eyelids twitch as I sit beside her bed, watching as she rouses herself from the nightmares that hold her prisoner most of the time.

I've had a hard time feeling sorry for someone like her. But when I see how she's ripped the hair from her balding scalp and how frail she's become, I realize this is no longer Madame. That woman died the day we battled over Craewick.

She opens her mouth three or four times before saying, "You were broken, Julietttta," so quietly I barely hear her, but there's a question in her voice, something which appears to haunt her.

How did you do this?

"Do you know who came . . . to see me? Braaay," she says, pulling in a trembling breath. "I thought he would . . . kill . . ." She pauses, grimacing. "'There has been enough death in Craewickkk,' he said." A thin laugh escapes her, followed by a series of rattling coughs. "I ordered that Minder to slit his brother's throat and he is too weeeak to do anything about it." She clutches the sheet with gnarled fists and grinds her teeth.

The nurses say that she does this often. Moments of coherency followed by episodes where she shivers uncontrollably, her skin icy to the touch. Eventually, she'll fall into a coma. And then all the history of Craewick, all those memories from rulers of old, will be locked up inside her. We all agree it's time to start anew.

Her eyes roll back before she says in a voice lower than her own, "Weakness is perceiving a threat and doing nothing to stop it."

I draw closer, her words identical to ones in my memory of when my mother was first placed in this bed.

Her voice changes to one I recognize, heard every week from the auction block. "Yes, Father."

"Threats are only threats if you allow them to flourish. Seek and destroy," says the lower voice.

"Oh, I've already found my greatest threat," says Madame. "And I plan to destroy it."

"Who?" answers the lower voice.

"You," she whispers.

A chill runs down my spine as I watch Madame's memories play out, remembering what my grandfather said when we first spoke of her condition.

"She's reliving a variety of things, her memories muddled with those from generations of other Craewick rulers. Most of the time, she cries out to her father, calling him weak and vowing she'll never be looked upon the same way. Were you aware that he was murdered?"

"She told me herself," I say.

He looks at Madame. "Well, we've finally discovered who his murderer was."

Widening my eyes, I gasp. "She killed her own father?"

"Our past has a way of finding us, doesn't it? Now she's caught in the memory of that night, experiencing the horror she committed over and over again," Grandfather says. *"The more I watch her, seeing all these memories trapped inside her, I've come to believe that Madame spent her whole existence trying to become something she wasn't . . . and never became anyone at all."*

I wait until Madame breaks free from her memories, her bloodshot eyes shifting back and forth. Her gaze lingers on my necklace until it meets mine.

"I came to tell you that you were right about me. For four years, my Gift terrified me. I'd seen how it could be used for evil just as easily as for good. My heart was broken, but when you tried to destroy my family, you pieced it back together stronger than I ever imagined it could be." I lean in close and whisper, "You gave us the power we needed to destroy you."

She screams as I walk away, but I don't look back. Madame belongs to the past now.

On my way to the square, I pass the woodworkers designing the newest addition to Craewick—the gardens. I wave to a few of my old neighbors working alongside a group of former Hollows. They're building greenhouses and arboretums alongside the new shops, and the sweet scent of pine sparks memories of being in the woods out-side of Aravid with Reid.

It'll be springtime before our shipments of Aravid flowers arrive, but Grandfather is more than willing to stay until the job is finished. I'm glad for any excuse to keep him around a bit longer, and Commander Averett has volunteered to watch over the Woodland Realm while he's gone.

It's as crowded as Auction Day in the square, but things couldn't be more different. There are children laughing, adults chitchatting as Bray and Beau handle the adoptions to get the orphans and younger Shadows into new homes. It's a sight I know Joss, an orphan herself who found a family with the Shadows, would love.

Grinning, I sidestep a girl with red ringlets and a spatter of freckles skipping over to a family with four children already. As I watch her giggling with her new brothers and sisters, I see glimpses of my old friend. Of the courage Joss found after losing her family and the joy she discovered in becoming part of another. She proved the hardest things in life will either break us or give us a strength we never knew we had.

All around me are Gifted, Ungifted, and those too young to know standing side-by-side, skin touching skin. There's color in their cheeks and in their outfits—no longer gray, stiff, and high-necked.

"Joy is rarely found in anything other than sharing

life together," my grandfather told me days ago. "Madame threatened her people with auctions and the Maze, but threats aren't what brought harmony to this city. Friendships did."

Unfortunately, not everyone's interested in a new kind of unity. Though the majority of Minders have pledged to the alliance between Porter, Sorien, and Bray, the ones who refused have been sent to Kripen. But my grandfather and Felix have made it clear the removal and implantation of memories isn't a method they're interested in. With Declan imprisoned, Felix has taken over command in Kripen for now, and though his prisoners won't be hunted down and tortured, they will be kept there until their memories clear them of any future ill intent.

Even in a sea of people, Bray has already spotted me when I meet his stare. He nods briefly as I raise my hand. Our relationship is one I've yet to name. Friendship doesn't sound right, though I can't deny there's a bond. Certain memories, especially ones of Cade, shared only between the two of us. Nowadays he spends most of his time with Beau. Bray lost one brother but has been reunited with another.

I step inside my grandfather's house, once the treasury, that's now been rebuilt into one of many colorful rowhomes. People scurry in and out, carrying shiny platters piled high with sweets and delicacies for the festivities beginning at sunset in the square. I spy Ryder plucking candies off a passing tray and grin, grateful the only kind of thieving she does nowadays gives her nothing more than a stomachache.

Reid brushes up beside me. "Take a walk before the party?"

We wind up on a hill overlooking Craewick, the sun spilling orange light and warmth over the city. I tell him about Madame, how my fear of her return has vanished, as we sit and lean back on our elbows.

The lanterns my grandfather had mounted on every street corner are lit one-by-one, and the square glitters like the darkening night sky, countless candles flickering in the soft wind. Even from here, we hear the ripples of laughter and the soft rumble of conversation as the celebration begins below.

A tear slips down my cheek before I wipe it away.

Reid laces his fingers through mine, his skin warm and tingling.

"I can't help but wonder why Madame gets to live while so many died. But when I saw her face, twisted with agony . . . I think Grandfather is right. I don't think she's ever lived at all." I touch Penn's band on Reid's wrist, remembering when my grandfather told me that we must live for something higher than ourselves. "I see the kind of life I want in the love my parents found together. In how my mother never lost hope, even when all the odds were stacked against her. In how my grandfather and Felix are able to create beauty out of nothing. In the unwavering loyalty of Joss, Cade, and even Bray." I look at him. "In the bond that will never be lost between you and Penn."

Reid inches closer. "Do you ever think about what would've happened if you never left the Shadows?"

"Every day," I say quietly.

"I wish Cade, Joss, and Penn were here, and your father was with your mother. But if I'd never left my family and if you'd never left the Shadows . . . without that pain and anguish, all this," he spreads his hands out wide toward the lively square, "wouldn't have been possible."

"Do you know who used to tell me things like that?" I nudge him gently. "Penn."

His face lights up. "Really?"

"I remember this one time, we got stuck in this terrible storm out in the woods. I was in a bad mood—"

"You, really?"

I grin. "It finally stopped raining right before this incredible sunset, and Penn said, 'That's what I love about rain,' and I grumbled something in annoyance, of course, but then he said 'Sunsets are ten times prettier after a storm. They're proof that good can come out of something bad.' I'm not sure I ever really believed him."

"And now?" Reid asks.

"Now I think the pain of losing someone I love should only make me love harder and deeper. That seeing the evil of the world should only make me cling more tightly to the good," I say. "That it's not the hardships of the past that define us, but the strength we find in overcoming them."

"Together," adds Reid.

I take his hand.

As dusk fades into night, we stay up on the hill, sharing memories about Penn and the Shadows, of my childhood in Blare and his with the Tribes, all the while making new ones together. And when he leans in and kisses me, I know whatever joys the past holds, the ones we've yet to discover will be even better.

And once every crumb of cake has been eaten and our feet grow sore from dancing all night, we remember those we've lost and toast the ones who live in memory of them, celebrating together as Craewick begins anew. I smile as my grandfather wraps his arms around my mother and sister, drawing them closer. With Reid's hand in mine, I look up at the sunrise, a string of words playing on my lips as the starry sky blooms with the color of a new day.

Better things await me.

ACKNOWLEDGMENTS

This is a story that's very near to my heart, and I'm incredibly thankful to each and every reader for giving me the chance to share it. There are so many people who've supported and encouraged me throughout this entire journey, all of which have gone above and beyond anything I ever expected.

From the bottom of my heart, I'd also like to thank:

Steve Malk: I'm constantly in awe of your passion for stories and storytellers, and this book would not exist apart from your insight, encouragement, and excitement. Thank you for helping me find my voice and for how tirelessly you worked to bring this story to life. You're the best agent anyone could ever ask for, and I'm forever grateful for you.

Hannah Mann: From day one, your enthusiasm for

this story has amazed me. Your constant kindness and unwavering support has had a lasting impact on me, and you've played an irreplaceable role in the creation of this book. I'm so thankful you've been there every step of the way.

Thank you both for not only walking alongside me on this writing journey but also for your wonderful friendship.

Lauren Spieller: When you selected me to be on your team for Pitch Wars, I was absolutely thrilled. Your sharp editorial eye and insightful feedback proved to be invaluable. Thank you for being such a fantastic mentor during the contest and for your advice and excitement since then.

Annette Bourland: Thank you for making my dream come true. Your vision and zeal for this story means the world to me. I feel truly privileged that you acquired this book, and I can't thank you enough for connecting me with the perfect editor.

Hannah VanVels: What a pleasure it's been to work with you. I've felt your love for this story from the first moment we spoke, and to have you as my editor, and now my friend, is a tremendous gift. You've given me endless amounts of fantastic insight, and I'm so lucky to have had you by my side during this entire process.

Mary Hassinger, Jennifer Hoff, and the entire Blink Team: It's an honor to work alongside you. Your passion for books is contagious, and I couldn't have asked for a better experience than the one you've given me. Thank you for all that you do.

Dad, Jacob, Jenna, Sawyer, Mason, Granny, the rest of my incredible family, and friends: You're my greatest source of joy and inspiration, and I'm so proud to be your daughter, sister, aunt, granddaughter, niece, cousin, and friend. I could spend a hundred years thanking you for your love and support, and still, it would only skim the surface of what I feel for you all. I love you dearly.

Mom: You've taught me more about life than I can ever express. Even when the odds were against you, you never lost hope and your joy never wavered. Witnessing your deep-rooted courage is what made me want to share this story, and to place this book in your hands is an incredible blessing and a memory I'll never forget. I love you.

THE MEMORY THIEF
DISCUSSION QUESTIONS

1. What is the purpose of each of the Four Realms? What kinds of resources are found in each Realm? How do they support one another?

2. There is a big division between the Gifted and the Ungifted. What are some of the advantages of being Gifted? What are some of the disadvantages? How are the Ungifted treated by the other people groups and leadership in the Realms?

3. In Etta's society, memories hold the highest value. What kinds of things hold the highest value in your society/community? In your family?

4. Throughout the Four Realms, there are individuals known as Hollows. How does a person become a Hollow? What are the risks of housing too many foreign memories?

5. While individuals can purchase memories at the Memory Auction, there are also ways to erase painful memories. Do you think it's a good idea to erase memories? In what ways do your memories make up who you are as a person?

6. Before Etta returns to the Shadows, she says, "It's always a risk to play with memories, when you can't help but sink into a sea of others' wishes, hopes, and dreams . . ." What are some of the reasons Etta is scared about returning to the Shadows? Why does Etta worry about becoming a memory thief?

7. The motto of the Shadows is "To help those who can't help themselves." How did Greer's vision for the Shadows differ from Bray's? Would you consider one a better leader than the other?

8. Etta wears four leather bracelets. What do these bracelets symbolize for her?

9. While speaking to Madame, Etta says, "I only stole what never belonged to your citizens in the first place and gave the memories back to their rightful owners. It's your job to protect the Ungifted, but if you won't, then the Shadows will." In what ways does Etta live by her own rule of only stealing to help others? Is there a point when she breaks

the rule? If so, how does it affect her and those around her?

10. What is a Ghost, and what is their purpose in this society? Who are the Hunters, and how are they affected by the kinds of memories they choose to steal?

11. Etta possesses many admirable qualities such as her bravery, cleverness, and dedication to her family. But these qualities can also turn into her flaws. At what points in the story do we see traits like these hindering Etta from reaching her goals? How do they inform her character growth? Why is it important for readers to meet characters like Etta?

12. In what ways do the obstacles within the Maze reflect Etta's inner struggles?

13. At the beginning of the story, Etta is crippled with guilt about her mother's accident. How has her perspective on the past changed by the end of the book?

14. How are the themes of forgiveness and mercy shown throughout the story?

15. If you could buy any memory or talent, what would you choose? Why?

A NOTE FROM
LAUREN MANSY

Long before this story was written, it was a memory of mine.

When I was around Etta's age, my mom was diagnosed with a heart condition, which led to an unexpected open-heart surgery. Before she was rushed into the operating room, my mom's heart had stopped six times. The doctors warned my family that due to the trauma she'd experienced, there was a possibility that my mom wouldn't remember us, when or even if she woke up.

So we waited to see if the same joyful woman who'd gone into surgery would be the same woman who survived it.

I was sitting at her bedside when she first began to stir after her surgery. She slipped in and out of consciousness and couldn't speak because of her breathing tube. But as I touched her hand, she wrapped hers around mine and squeezed it three times, our signal that meant *I love you*. It was a moment I'll never forget! In that tiny gesture, she'd spoken the words she couldn't yet say. And I knew, much like Etta, that my mom was coming back to me.

On my mom's road to healing, there were many tears, setbacks, and days of wondering if things would ever return to the way they had once been. But my mom never lost hope. Witnessing her recovery showed me that there are heroes all around us. I never knew how much courage there could be in taking one little step, then two. How much happiness is found as family, friends, even strangers prove to be such faithful allies. How much love can be expressed in three tiny squeezes. It was during these times of waiting, uncertainty, and in the joy of my mom waking up that the seeds of this story were planted. But overall, it was her unfailing courage that would become the true inspiration for *The Memory Thief*.

When I first began writing about this experience, I wasn't always sure how to express what I'd felt when faced with the possibility of losing my mom. Some worries and fears were too difficult for me to say out loud, but through telling Etta's story, I began to better understand my story. It gave me a voice whenever I struggled to find my own and proved to be a source of healing that I'm incredibly grateful to have found.

Writing this book has been an incredible journey, and I can't ever thank you enough for allowing me to share it with you.

THE FOUR REALMS

THE BLARIEN SE

THE COASTAL REALM

BLARE

THE DESERT REALM

KRIPEN

THE BLARIE